Coastal Healing

Coastal Healing

BRUCE GRAHAM

Purple Porcupine Publishing
P.O. Box 555, Stewiacke, NS B0N 2J0
Purpleporcupine.ca

Editor: Penelope Jackson

Library and Archives Canada Cataloguing in Publication

Title: Coastal healing / Bruce Graham.
Names: Graham, Bruce (Bruce W.), author.
Description: Includes bibliographical references.
Identifiers: Canadiana (print) 20250170299 | Canadiana (ebook) 20250 174022 | ISBN 9781738899579
  (softcover) | ISBN 9781738899586 (EPUB)
Subjects: LCGFT: Novels.
Classification: LCC PS8613.R3431 C63 2025 | DDC C813/.6—dc23

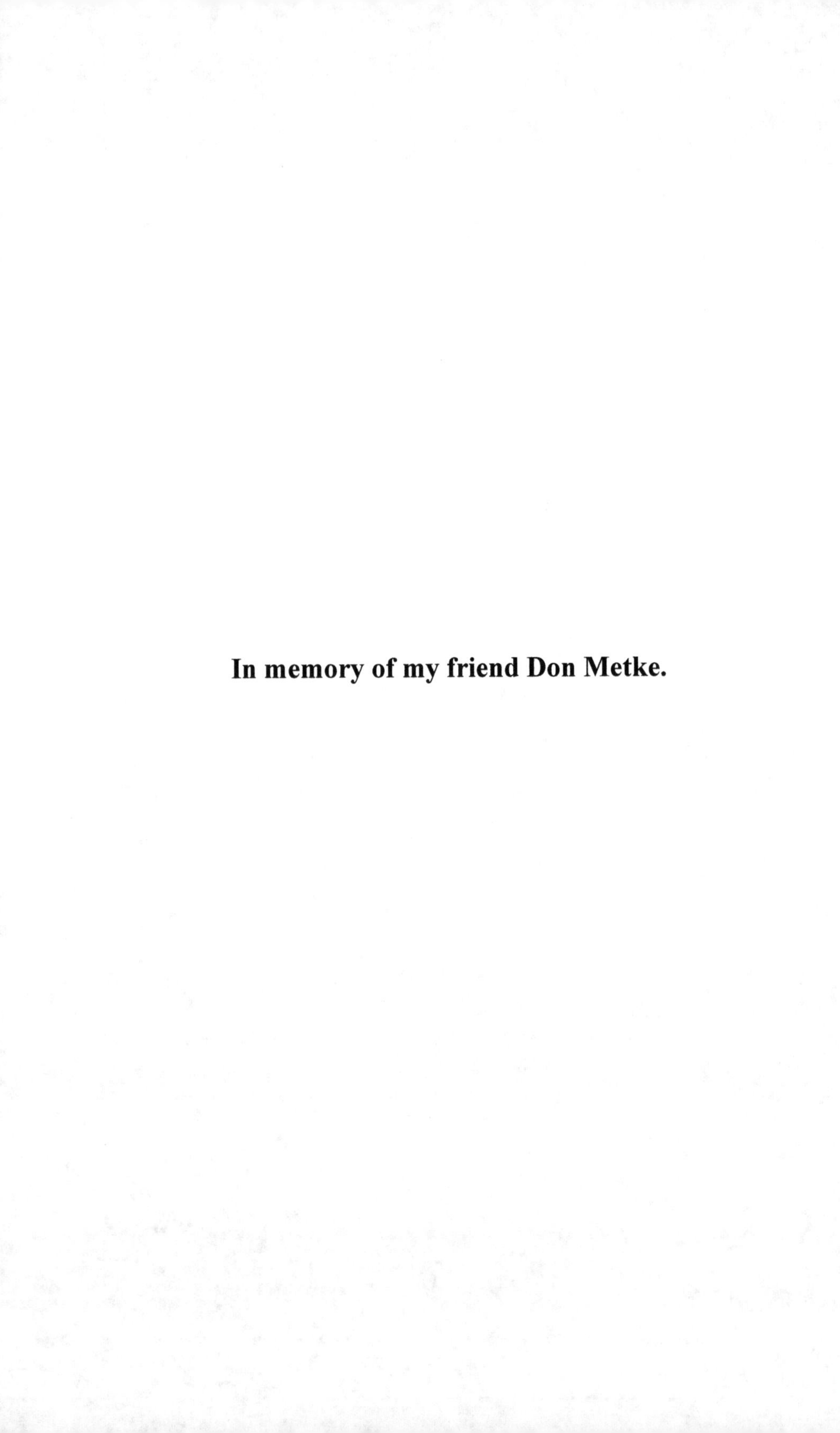

In memory of my friend Don Metke.

TABLE OF CONTENTS

Life is altered when you live on the coast. It is more intricate with one eye on the water. Coastal living dictates such an observance because the water reveals the world at the lip of the ocean. The coast is the place where nature's worlds collide. It can be an edgy world when the water is winning, and the water is always winning. The coast is a dangerous place at times, where footing must be careful and respect for mother ocean always required to save the one life you were given.

But there is the therapeutic side too, where the rush of water soothes the soul. The coast can be a place of healing.

Preface

There are few sandbars in the world that warrant special mention in an atlas. But there it is, the Apple River Bar on page thirty-six of *The Nova Scotia Atlas: Sixth Edition.*

Perhaps its fame is due to its unique geological position, between a tidal marsh that is a bay twice a day and a real bay, called Chignecto, one of the arms of the mighty Bay of Fundy. Maybe its prominence is because of its past economic significance. The Bar was once the hub of commercial activity. Millions of board feet of lumber were shipped down Apple River when it was high on sea water.

My father lumbered in Apple River before I was born. I was about five years old the first time I stood on the Bar. The next time I was in my early teens. My magical feeling in those times I transferred to Lester in this book. The people are fictional, yet, as we know, fiction is never totally imagined. An element of truth worms its way into this story.

The Bar is wider in the middle now than years ago. Higher tidewaters push more sand and gravel onto this sliver of land half a mile long, less than a third of that wide. A few skinny spruce claim the centre high ground.

A few things about the names. "The shore" refers to the Parrsboro Shore that runs, if you want to stretch it, from Apple River to Parrsboro, the road running along two coasts of the Bay of Fundy, the Minas Channel and Basin, and Chignecto Bay.

The community is named Advocate Harbour; locals shorten it to Advocate or, if they're wistful, the harbour.

I capitalize the Bar due to my deep respect for it and its history. The "Cape" in "Cape Islander" is pronounced "cap," as though there were no "E." Tossed between French and English for a couple of centuries, that's just the way it is. As both spellings are in print, I choose not to put an apostrophe in Spensers Island.

This is the coast known as Chignecto, one of the two fingers of the Bay of Fundy, and this is where our story starts…and it starts with laughter: A dozen men are bent over killing themselves, and you can hear them in the woods above the shore. Lester's neighbours are on the Chignecto beach having a hell of a good time, standing around in a clump watching him and his salvage job. Later, dry and warm, Lester would laugh too, claiming they were all half drunk. That was an exaggeration. Sure, a nip went around, but after all it was a borrowed tractor, belonging to one of the onlookers, who had mixed feelings about the sanity of the venture but was trying his best to put on a happy face.

There had been debates while they stood together as to where the old house came from. The consensus was it floated across the bay from New Brunswick, on the other shore of Chignecto Bay. Tides are higher, storms are worse, and soft ground is getting weaker. It wasn't the first or the last home of many generations to fall into the sea.

Now, Lester was trying to pull one out of the tide, and it was a risky venture, but they understood why Lester had acted when he did. The wind had swung the old structure around, blowing it on shore; it got fetched up in the natural elevation of the beach. Before the tide turned, Lester acted, getting things organized, but it took time; the tide was ahead of him already, and where it placed the derelict building in one tide, it could snatch it away in the next. The wind was bringing in water heavy. Lester was racing against the ocean with the wheels of the tractor half buried in seawater. His brother-in-law Cliff was up to his chest. He had lost the connection the first time. Lester and Cliff were both struggling; if they were smaller men they might have been swept away, but both stood above six feet, and weighed over two hundred pounds, and they had withstood the force of the water while connecting the cable to the strapping they'd wrapped around the battered old dwelling. The water was rolling now, the wind blowing right into them. The neighbours watching had suddenly gone quiet. Not until they were back on the tractor and almost up on the beach did they dare to breathe, but when half the back end suddenly came off in one broken, soggy piece, they went into hysterics. The best party of the season. The tractor survived too.

Lester positioned his shack on the half-mile-long Bar, exactly where he planned, on what little high ground there was in the middle of the Bar. He nestled it down between the skinny spruce trees so it wouldn't move much.

He called it his float house. It floated in with the tide, and if a hurricane didn't whack it to pieces, it might go out in the same manner. There was no question the tides were getting higher, climbing over the environment year by year, creeping salty fingers taking more of the land.

Chapter 1

Coastal Lessons

Lester Hatfield always claimed the Apple River Bar was magical in moonlight. The way the colour of things changed, driftwood became pearl white, beach rocks took on a blue nuance. He taught his children to watch the seawater. It was a gauge of the weather to come. It could be, at various times, black as ink or silver as a serving set. It could be forty shades of blue and green. When the sky turned inhospitable, the bay turned gray and brown. It could change within minutes, transformed from dark to light to shiny reflections of the sky, and plopped with a drop or two of gold.

Lester had taught his children and their friends to look for colour in every aspect of life, especially here at the Bar, where every aspect of life was just shaded slightly differently. There were long walks along the shore. Lester instructed his children to study the cliffs because there was danger there, particularly in springtime. He told them the difference between the minerals on the beach and where to find mica and fool's gold, to recognize gypsum and sandstone, slate and granite.

Heather was one of those children he had instructed and reared since the age of seven. She had come back to the Bar recently to heal and find herself again, as she had done the year she lost her mother. Heather wasn't Lester's child exactly, but she might just as well have been. He had raised her, taught her what he taught his own daughter and his other niece.

"Look for things hidden, found upon investigation," he told them. "There is a personal reward in finding something precious but hidden."

He told them that people were often blind to their surroundings as they pass through life. "Don't be one of those people. Your eyes are hardly necessary if you don't look. Life is an exploration, make it so. So many have eyes but they walk through life and see nothing. Never stop searching or investigating the world around you."

He did nature walks into the woods with them, his disabled son and the girls walking behind as a cluster of ducklings. He showed them the difference in mushrooms, where to find the tasty chanterelles and the small white field mushrooms, and if he found a poisonous species, such as the rare evening nightshade, he explained what would happen if they ate one. That was where Heather and her cousins learned the importance of the outdoors, the testament of nature and the natural world around them. Lester went out of his way about the dangers too. Why the cliffs became unstable in the springtime. Which plants would give you a rash if they were touched. He took them up the Chignecto coast to where they could find fool's gold in the rocks, and there was always a competition over who could find the biggest chunk of the shiny pyrite.

Lester taught them the coast, too, taking them in his lobster boat to the headlands of Green Point and Squally Point. He taught them the bays, the dotted inlets along the coast, Seal Cove, Andersons and Spencer Cove.

More than anything, Lester emphasized the tides, because Chignecto was a coast of high, rolling tides. Turn your back and you can be trapped. He stressed the importance of knowing where the water was at any given time. Walk out at low tide, just fooling around, playing in a tidal pool or attempting to slide on the mud flats, and the tide can surround you. If you feel it on your ankles and pay no attention because you're having fun catching eels and looking for crabs under rocks then, he told them, the water is rapidly accompanied by a surprising heavy fog bank. Suddenly you can't see the beach and the water is up to your waist and rising swiftly. You are blanketed by fog, and you can't see anything. You are suddenly afraid, and when you call out for help your voice is muffled by the vapour. You take a few steps but can't tell if you are walking into the bay or towards the beach. Anyone who has experienced such an encounter knows the meaning of sheer terror.

They asked him once if it had happened to him. "Twice. When I was a lad my dad heard me the first time so it wasn't so bad. The other was when I was sixteen, it was terrifying."

It was too terrible to talk about, and he said nothing more. If it wasn't his words that convinced them to ask no further questions, it was the look in his eyes and his voice that told them.

"Always the tides," he said, "relentless, never still. Remember, it's a lot of water moving in and out of the Bay of Fundy, every hour of every day, and it's never as serene as it appears. That constant motion could kill you if you failed to notice its withdrawing and advancing. The tide can be as quiet as a sleeping choirboy or a rolling wall of angry water. "It is in our blood," Lester told them. "We live next to it, shoulder to shoulder. Always respect it."

Heather was thinking of those lessons standing on the shore in the gathering darkness, feeling the draw of beach and bay: things she'd missed terribly in recent years in a lonely time in a part of the world without water, tide, or beach.

The others had gone up to the house. Gert was cold and cranky, telling Marg they were both going to freeze to death if they didn't get inside. Lester had gone ahead to light a fire in the kitchen stove and put on some coffee. Heather walked alone, gathering wood for the next bonfire. This one was the first of the season, early, but warm for May.

She breathed in the sea air, something she had longed for and dreamed about in that damnable desert, that land of stone and sand, rock and grief. It was a world with little hope for women. Even Canadian female soldiers were looked at and pointed at by local men as being some strange anomaly.

She often felt the need to be alone, and what better place than right here at the Bar, with the moon in full face, giving the beach rocks that particular colour and putting silver fingers on the advancing tide?

The east wind had come up in the last half hour, making little swells rolling high towards the shore. She knew where to stand exactly, where the very edges of the tide touched her toes. Heather slipped off her sandals and stepped up to her ankles. It was a cooling sensation she had longed for many times in recent years. She could call up even the memory of it, the sensation, from thousands of miles away, be it in a desert tent or a fractious dorm. Very often in the heat of day and the chill of the night, she had made herself imagine the seawater touching her toes. Such strong affection for this place made her cry. She knew that was no way for a soldier to act. A shiver went through her, familiar by this time, not because of the water; it was a symptom of what she considered her poor decisions. Heather had learned to ignore the tremor; let it run its course, she was told, down her legs, up her spine, only bad now when it reached her neck, which thankfully had only happened a few times in the month Heather had been home.

She gave one final, searching scan of the coming tide and the far bank of Apple River Bay, that little tidal bay on the other side of the Bar. The float house faced this small body of water that twice a day was not water at all, but a mud flat. Across this gorge, the trees on the other bank were only silhouettes against a withering garnet sky. Heather took a deep breath of the sea air. To her back, on the other side of the Bar, the bigger, wider Chignecto Bay ran down the coast until it spilled into the Gulf of Maine and the gulf ended up in the Atlantic Ocean. It was sea air, all right, all the way from the billowing deeps. The tide was coming and bringing the cooler atmosphere that made Gert gripe and twist her sweater around her. Heather took another deep breath and turned back to the float house.

Chapter 2

Childhood Dreams

Since childhood, Heather had loved the feel of sea mist on her face. Her mother died during their last visit here, and Heather had been with Lester ever since. Her memory before the age of seven was disjointed, piecemeal. She remembered a birthday party or a picnic or special something, but where it was and with whom, she didn't know. Just her mother, changing jobs or men or cities. They moved a lot, her mother dragging her from one place to another, from one home to another. Was that why she had such a strong attraction to Apple River and the Bar? They were permanent, although Lester said they weren't, telling her more than once that nothing was permanent and never would be. "Look," he said, "and you'll see the changes."

She had replied, "But this is the only place I really remember as a child. There are such solid memories here. So, I considered it permanent. I have been here in the summer and in our house in Advocate in the winter since I was seven. That, in my life, spells permanency."

This indeed was her family. She had grown up with Lester's son, Gus, a young man with Down syndrome; Lester's daughter, Boots, big boned like her father and more fun than anybody Heather had ever known. Cliff and Gert's only daughter, Marg, was petite with dark eyes and hair. She was the quietest of the group. A little more studious, a little less noisy. She played every game growing up with them, ran around the beach, splashed and swam in Apple River Bay, whose more shallow, tidal water was always warmer than the larger Chignecto with its more open water. Marg played with the others but did so with quiet caution. She was never as reckless as Boots and Heather.

That's how it was before Boots went to university to be a veterinarian and Marg left for teachers college. Always together, Heather and Marg were often mistaken for sisters, and over time they considered themselves as such. These were the people in Heather's life, and this was the beach that restored her years ago. Slowly healed her sorrow, so she could think of her mother without crying. That took a full summer, but it worked. As a result, there was always an immense comfort by the water, the briny smells of seaweed and clam shells, the squawk of herring gulls dipping and dropping above the waves.

Heather heard the heat before she felt it, the crackling of dry driftwood, its snapping and popping like violent popcorn. Lester had such a roaring fire going, the front door was wide open. It was rustic inside; lanterns glowed, giving a soft light to Gert and Marg sitting at the kitchen table drinking coffee. Lester and Cliff were standing by the counter holding glasses of rum. Gus was sitting on the wood box, drinking chocolate milk. The room had the aroma of coffee and warm chocolate. Gert had prepared chocolate cookies at home and brought them here to bake in the oven. "They taste better and cook faster in a hot wood stove," she said.

That was one of Gert's directions for life, of which there were many. When Heather walked in on them, Gert was telling her husband she didn't believe a word of what he was saying and wished he would stop with his tall tales because people were thinking he was crazy.

"You know why I know that's not true?" Gert said. "We would have heard about it."

"Nobody was particularly eager to talk about it," Clifford retorted. "The guy who went through the window was highly embarrassed. The family involved are quiet people, never wanting to make a fuss."

"No one along the Parrsboro Shore is that quiet," Gert snapped and gave one of her derisive, mocking snorts, frequently employed at bridge games when her partner made what Gert considered an unwise bid.

Marg told her parents it was time to go, but Clifford wasn't ready to relinquish his position as chief storyteller.

"I was there," Clifford said, ignoring both wife and daughter because there was more laughter to squeeze out of Lester and Gus and now Heather too, who hadn't heard the entire story. Clifford was prepared to defend the veracity of one of his stories when challenged. "I was there" was the common retort.

According to Cliff, a young chap with not much experience was paragliding, where people catch air drafts off the cliffs with a sail. If they're good at it, they can stay afloat for hours. According to Clifford, the young fella was somewhere between Port Greville and Parrsboro catching the winds, when something went terribly wrong. It was late afternoon, and he was getting ready to call it quits when this rogue wind hit him so suddenly, he was helpless. He could see the lights of the farmhouse as he was hurtling towards it. The young aeronaut both praised his helmet and prayed to his God as he went through the front window. He declared later he distinctly remembered the aroma of fresh cornbread as he slid across the dining room table just as the entire family of eight had completed their grace, thankful for the food they were about to receive when the unexpected guest arrived. "Dear God in Heaven," Clifford declared, "the family in the house, well, you should have seen the mashed potatoes and pickles in the air when this young fella smashed through the dining room window, feet first, with such a thunderous noise the lady of the house grabbed the roast chicken off the platter and held it to her breast as if it was an infant before she dropped to the floor in a dead faint. The older boys thought it was an air raid, that war had finally come to Parrsboro Shore. They scrambled to reach under their beds for their guns. The younger ones, mop-haired little rascals, just disappeared by sliding off their chairs and under the table as if their bones were rubber.

"It was something to see," Clifford declared, seeing his daughter take her fiddle out of the case but not surrendering his story just yet.

"That young fella sailed through the window and slid across the table, clearing dishes, silverware, a water pitcher, and anything else that happened to be in his way."

"That's ridiculous, I don't believe a word of it," Gert said, and Marg put her fiddle to her chin, final number, she said, telling her parents the evening was concluding.

"Who was the guy and what happened?" asked Gus, filling his glass again. He had often considered parasailing but had never attempted it.

"Guy from Parrsboro, forget his name, but nothing happened. I think he paid for the window and wrote the family a nice letter of apology and that was that," Clifford said.

"That's just silly nonsense, and it never happened, and you know it," Gert told her husband.

"Would I make up something like that?" Clifford asked, looking rather dejected when he received a rousing chorus of "YES."

Marg played a Scottish dirge, soft and slow, and that musical magic drifted out the door of the float house and down the beach, where people in trailers farther along the Bar turned down their radios just to listen. A hush fell on the far bank of Apple River Bay as the owls and nighthawks were stilled.

Heather wanted a quick word with Marg alone, but maybe this wasn't the time. She waited until they were putting on their coats and gathering up things from the beach.

"What are you up to tomorrow?" she called as Marg was at the door. "You home?"

"Yes, I've got some papers to correct for an hour or so. Are you coming down?"

"Yes, after lunch," Heather replied. They were first cousins and friends since childhood. Marg was a few months older and had been teaching school for several years. It had been their life plan, hatched eons ago when they were eight. They would be schoolteachers beyond doubt or hesitation; teaching was their chosen career path already laid out in young minds. Later, with adolescent fantasy in full flight, they promised each other to work in the same school, marry brothers, and live next door to each other.

Neither woman had lived up to those childish expectations, but Margaret had come closest. She had at least gone to teachers college. Heather was to follow but at the last minute chose not to.

By the time she completed high school, Heather was certain she could not fulfill her childhood commitment. She hated the very thought of a life in a classroom, or an office for that matter. She liked the freedom of the outdoors. She was a good student and had already been accepted into the teaching program for the coming September, but that little voice refused to stop asking questions she couldn't answer. What did she really want in life? Damn it, she didn't know. It was a feeling she couldn't explain, could not account for, couldn't quite put her finger on the why of things, but she yearned for something other than teaching. Maybe it was just life itself calling her out of the shadows. Who hadn't heard such a call, telling them, almost baiting them to do something crazy, like join the Foreign Legion? Most ignore such fleeting urges; few are willing to follow such passing fancies into the unknown.

But a few do. Heather did, not once but twice.

Chapter 3

Failure

Gus and Lester had finally put the engine back together by late the next morning. The Cape Islander was ready for the water. Heather came down before lunch with a thermos of coffee to help out. She was mechanically inclined, good with her hands, and she assisted them in pulling the old Briggs & Stratton apart.

"I'm almost done," Gus said, taking the pre-offered coffee.

"I want to see you prime it, then we'll know, won't we?" Heather replied.

"You coming out with us?"

"No, I can't today. I told Marg I'd go up after lunch."

"Know what you're going to do yet?" Gus asked in his usual blunt manner.

"No, I'm looking at my options. Isn't that what they call it?"

"Which means what?" Gus asked.

"I guess scanning around for possibilities. I suppose it's something to say when you get tired of all the questions you can't answer. It depends a lot on what the military says when I get my release papers and medicals."

"Far as I'm concerned you can stay right here with Lester and me, just like before." Gus got busy bailing after that comment, refusing to meet Heather's smile.

Gus had always been sweet on Heather. He liked Marg, but Heather was the object of his affection. Heather wished at times he would do more to conceal it.

She went back to the float house thinking about the past, when Boots was still with them, how lively things were. Now it was quiet all the time.

Gus was thinking similar thoughts watching her walk up the beach. He wished she would smile more and be happy. He and his father both told her to cheer up. "The world isn't such a bad place," Lester said.

That's what he thought, and she embraced him for it. But Heather knew that apart from one year at a cloistered American school, Lester had spent his entire life within twenty miles of where he stood today. He had never seen things she had witnessed. Call it man's inhumanity to man, if you will. Even thinking of those memories caused that tremble, the rippling window blind up and down her legs and spine.

Lester was a man who always saw the best in people, even people who cheated him or wronged him in some manner. Except for Angus and a few others, Lester was not a grudge holder, but he detested thieves. He wasn't stupid either. In his youth he had been a good student, had gone to Bible college in New York. That was his year away. The family assumed Lester would enter Mount Allison University, get his degree, and become a minister. He did none of those things. He came back to Advocate Harbour and married the girl he had always loved. They stayed put. Lester learned the plumbing business, most of which he already knew. He was Heather's uncle, her mother's older brother. Heather would never destroy Lester's illusion, but there were topics they needed to discuss, and she wondered, with Gussie down at the boat, was this the time? They were eating bacon and eggs, the usual Sunday lunch.

The tide was coming strong around the Bar in its twice daily swing. Full and foamy, the salty brine hitting the hot mud of the marsh changed the aroma and climate; even nature's sounds were transformed with the little ripple of waves, resembling the soft lapping of small dogs. The marsh was filling with water and becoming Apple River Bay.

Lester was in the kitchen when his battery clock reported it was noon hour. They were alone. Heather considered this would be a good time for them to talk. She thought about how to open the conversation. She wanted to tell him things; to make him understand she was not a coward. The blood and gore bothered them all, affected every member of the unit. She had stood up well to combat. If she owed anyone an explanation of why things had gone off the rails and why she had been turfed out of the army, it was him. Before she could put the right words together to bring up the subject, he interrupted her thinking.

"You and me, we're a lot alike," he told her across the table. "I didn't become a minister; you didn't become a schoolteacher."

"I don't know," Heather replied, choosing her words. "It was a mistake, everything I tried. I wanted suddenly at seventeen to be different. Different from Marg, maybe, different from other people. I thought I wanted something more meaningful. Look at me, I'm twenty-seven and I feel so unanchored somehow."

Of course, it was completely the wrong thing to say to Lester, who spent minutes, which suddenly seemed like very valuable minutes, pressing upon her the things she already knew: This was her home, she had her own room, Gus was not allowed in, no one was going to bother her. She was family.

In the time Lester was talking, if a person was trained and knew how, they could break down a C7, check for sand, prep, and reload. If a person knew how.

Heather came back to earth when she realized Lester had stopped. This was her chance.

"Yes, Lester, but the thing is, I'm hiding away. I'm hiding away like a criminal, but that's not what I am. I am not a criminal. I am a failure. One who cannot complete her mission. A criminal breaks the law, a failure simply fails."

"The last thing in the world you are is a failure. Not with what you've been through. You have to get past it somehow, child. I wish I could tell you how, I do, truthfully; I wish I knew the right words, but I'm not that smart."

Heather pressed her eyes tightly to stem anything that might be escaping. She understood she could cry freely now, cry when she wanted, whenever she needed it or just for the hell of it, without restriction. It was one of many freedoms she could now enjoy. She could cry without criticism, without being called names. "Crybaby" was one they used, accompanied by rude baby noises, amid high-pitched "Mommy, mommy," and the snickers, always the snickering. Snickering made her weak and others strong.

Gus arrived and the conversation ended. They took their coffee outside. The sun had turned the wave tops shiny as a new penny, but you had to catch it fast, only a split second at their very crest, before the golden tips of the waves disappeared and they rolled black and green again. The waves lapsed into millions of bubbles breaking on the beach pebbles. When he sat down Gus could read their expression; they had had a serious conversation. He knew his father was trying to bring Heather around, because she wasn't the same.

Lester said she was more down in the dumps. Gus knew that.

"Left a fun-loving girl, returned a serious woman," Gert said the other night. Gus, who never said much in a crowd, saw Marg physically shiver. The girls he had played with were happy and laughing; the women they'd grown into, well, Gus could see more than he said. Both Heather and Marg were restrained with each other, and with other people too. He and his father had talked about that, and Lester told him not to worry about Heather. Yet Gus knew his father was worried. It was all right for him to worry while telling his son not to? How was that right?

Chapter 4

Different Paths

The drive between Apple River and Spensers Island goes through Advocate Harbour, a coastal village renowned for scallop fishing, Acadian dykes, and delightful scenery. The fishing boats with gunnels painted green and blue were tied up on a Sunday with the hulls bobbing in the water as if greeting Heather as she crossed the village bridge. It was just a few miles down the road to Marg's.

What then? What to say? She wanted to get Marg away from Gert's grip and have a frank conversation. She had tried before, twice in the month she'd been home, but Marg seemed distant in some way.

To be truthful, Marg had hurt Heather during a vulnerable moment. Marg was the one person you could always depend on, but she hadn't been dependable at all. Emotionally she just hadn't been there for a friend in need. It hurt and it simmered. Partly because she and Marg had been like sisters and Heather felt just let down. Maybe because neither had a real sister, and they'd talked about that years ago when the bond between them was strong. Now there was energy missing in Marg's response to things, her reaction to people or events. There were no little seconds of inspiration or happiness on her face. Her eyes showed no indication of delight. Marg claimed she was fine. She was not married but had her students, they were her children, youngsters she released every summer for a new crop in the fall. She taught school, lived with her parents, never dated. Lester said Gert told him Marg hung back as if scared of something.

Heather had seen that herself since her return. It brought back memories of Marg in their childhood. Marg seemed to understand things, not in a childlike way, but more like an adult. Marg was never an energetic person, not like her and Boots and Gus, but she was happy. They were all happy once. Weren't they?

As Heather drew closer to Spensers Island, something started to roil inside her. It was, she knew from experience, anger. Anger at Marg for some reason. Marg, who Heather suddenly wanted to take down to the beach and give a good shaking to while demanding why a twenty-eight-year-old spinster was living in remote Spensers Island with her parents.

Marg in recent years was even more reserved. Heather had noticed that the last time she was home on leave. Such memories swirled through Heather's mind. Maybe *reserved* wasn't the word, but what was? Less smiling and less happy than she was years ago.

Heather felt responsible, maybe; at least for part of it. She knew her change of direction as a teenager had deeply wounded Marg, and driving, getting closer, Heather now felt accountable for the unhappiness of her lifelong friend.

Maybe that's when it all started, when Heather told Marg she wasn't going to teachers college but was going to Toronto to study art because they were young and should do something really crazy. She tried to whirl around crazy-like to demonstrate, but it fell flat. She never forgot the look Marg gave her, a hurt expression of loss, of being left out, of sudden abandonment. Heather didn't ask Marg to join her in Toronto, because Marg wouldn't have gone. She was more grounded, more set with things, but at seventeen Heather wasn't grounded and didn't want to be. She was setting herself on a different path, to follow her ability in the one thing that called her—painting. But was she good enough to be an artist? Lester said she was, and so did her high school friends. With Lester's praises in her ears and Boots chirping away about her great talent, Heather felt she had to give art a try. It was the only thing that really called her.

She was almost crying now as she drove into Spensers Island, a small cluster of houses, many from seafaring days because ships were built and sailed from this little coastal port. The waters were wide here by the opening of Chignecto Bay. And here was Heather Hatfield, once declared the prettiest girl in Advocate Harbour High School, crying so hard she could scarcely see the road. Sobbing like a madwoman, as if her memory had flushed years of Marg's life and happiness down the drain and Marg had never recovered. That's what it looked like to Heather. She remembered.

"Goddamn you, Heather. This was your dream too," Marg had said bitterly all those years ago. She didn't want to be a teacher either, she said in a fit of pique. But here she was, years later and still teaching, declaring she loved it now, but she didn't look like she loved anything.

We were children, we were dreamers. Why didn't she quit if she really didn't want to teach? Why am I carrying this load? That was anger inside the prettiest girl in high school, anger that was almost dangerous to her, like a drug she shouldn't be taking. It caused pain, grief, and nausea. That's what the army doctor told her, and the shrink agreed. "Control your emotions." Oh indeed, easily said. "Think positive things in times of stress. Be kind, not critical."

Heather really hoped Marg loved teaching as much as she professed to. They'd all said Marg would be a good teacher, especially for young children. She had the natural disposition of the patient teacher who seldom had to raise her voice. Loved by her little ones. Who didn't need any of her own, even if her own mother did. *Grandchildren have been a bone of contention between mother and daughter for some time. There's the teacher's pension, too, years down the road, but Marg looks like she's drying up now. She's not thirty and already talking about a pension, retirement, as if her entire career is just a big fucking ordeal.*

Heather pulled into the driveway of the neat little house, more high than wide, with natty gable windows on the second floor overlooking

Gert's gardens. It was some sort of replica of a lighthouse catering to Gert's taste, and an enlarged kitchen gave the lighthouse a swollen belly. People called it the pregnant lighthouse. Beyond the backyard, through a row of wispy evergreens, Heather could see the cove. The tide was midway, coming up the beach.

Marg met her at the door.

"Can we go for a walk?" Heather asked immediately, cutting off any small talk.

Marg simply nodded, rather gravely Heather thought, as if she was expecting something unpleasant but willing to take it or at least to hear it. Maybe Marg felt as Heather did, that they badly needed to reconnect, to reach out through the years and get back together somehow. That was what they required, some emotional warmth. Maybe Marg didn't know she needed it, but Heather knew.

Heather suddenly had that feeling again as they walked towards the beach. That uncertainness, the gnawing doubt she was wrong about everything. They hadn't changed; Gus was no smarter, Marg wasn't more withdrawn, Boots was probably still crazy, Gert was still sharp, age had only slowed her down a little. Clifford was still telling stories but was now paid to do so because of a grant received from the historical society for vocal storytelling. It was Heather who had changed. She was the outsider, part of the pattern of recent years. "Part of a pattern" were the words of her commanding officer when he handed over her papers. Medical leave for ninety days.

"Don't get attached to the word *leave*," he told her. "It's really a discharge, just time for the paperwork. You're out."

She saluted and was dismissed.

Walking between the trees in Marg's backyard, Heather thought to herself how quickly Marg had grabbed a jacket.

Marg wanted to talk too. *Be kind to her, be gentle*, Heather reminded herself; they had been friends, sisters, forever. Yet she felt neither kindness nor friendliness. Why were all Marg's troubles her troubles? Was she the root cause of Marg's unhappiness? The suspicion unsettled Heather: She had enough on her shoulders, and her sudden antagonistic feelings slightly frightened her. *Keep your emotions in control.*

They walked from mossy ground to beach gravel, a few steps into a different world. Side by side and without a word, they headed up the beach, away from the few early campers and the old canteen. The water always had a calming effect on Heather, and she needed it now.

Afghanistan might have been different if there had been beaches with water lapping on the shore. But there wasn't anything like that. It was landlocked, barren and brown, with dust the colour of cinnamon. Rocks and sand and tribal chiefs. She saw their customs and cruelty and little boys held tightly by tribal chiefs as their sexual toys. Women were denied an education or a voice in their communities. They were not permitted to drive a car and must keep covered in black garments in Afghanistan's stifling heat. The troops often saw the country as a culture stuck in the past. How much was she going to tell Marg, if Marg even asked? They had walked for three minutes without a word.

"So, how are you, Marg?" The question came out of Heather automatically to get the conversation going. She had a strong desire to move things along so the two of them could…what? Fix Marg? Is that what Heather was doing? Fixing her friend so the two of them could fix Heather? Patently stupid, she supposed, but she waited for Marg to speak.

"I'm fine, Heather. How are you doing?"

Marg was polite and distant, as if they were casual acquaintances. Heather closed her eyes and listened to the water. Inside she screamed for honesty, something Marg was now constantly withholding.

Heather bit her lip and opted for the truth.

"I'm a mess," she said and waited, but all she got from Marg was a polite "That's too bad," which didn't have a ring of sympathy to it. The reply was hollow just as Marg had become, as if she had been reamed out and only the shell remained.

"At least I told you the truth, as opposed to you saying you're fine."

"I *am* fine. What do you want me to say?"

"The truth would be nice," Heather responded. "If you're so fine, why do you look so goddamn unhappy all the time?"

"Did you learn to swear in the military? You never used to talk like that."

"Answer my question, Marg, stop deflecting the issue. I watched you last night at the float house. You did not look happy, and I know you, I know your moods. Answer my question, please. What's wrong?"

Marg stopped and met Heather's gaze. "What makes you think you know me, Heather? Because we hung out together as kids? I'm settled and content and you're the one who's unhappy with things, with decisions you've made."

"I saw things, Marg, terrible things, murder, mayhem, chaos. I performed well under fire, terrifying as it was, but it was my own troops, really. They didn't want a woman among them."

"That's too bad" came out of Marg's mouth again.

Heather wanted to shake her. "Yes, it is too bad. Now how about you, Marg? Why not unload your baggage on your old pal? I'm getting sick of this standoffish demeanour of yours."

Marg stopped and softly clasped Heather's arm. "Heather, there is nothing wrong with me. I'm content with my life."

"Aren't you lonely living with your parents, almost thirty, not married; are you even involved romantically? Not that it's any of my business." Heather could feel herself coming unglued, the ground beneath her feet, the beach stones moving in unison. Was Marg really holding her up? Was she out of control so completely?

Marg was steering her towards a driftwood log large enough for them to sit on. She took Heather's hand and squeezed it lightly.

"Don't you ever get horny?" Heather blurted out as a last gasp of defiance, and regretted it, or thought maybe she did.

"Is that more army talk?" Marg asked quietly.

"Yes." Heather sighed and stayed silent for a few seconds, looking intently at the incoming tide. Then she said, "I suppose so. I hardly know what's going to come out of my mouth next. I try to explain things to people, officers, friends, family, and I can't get anywhere."

"I was in a romance," Marg suddenly said, so quietly Heather wasn't certain she heard correctly.

"A love affair is how I would put it," Marg continued softly and slowly, while also watching the water. "It didn't work out."

"Is that why you're so sombre?" Heather asked without thinking. She had already relinquished control of the conversation. *Keep looking at the water*.

There was no wind, little ripples hardly noticeable pushed by the force of incoming billions of gallons of water. The bay was filling up, pale green fingers sliding ahead, silently climbing up the beach to rescue Heather.

"No," Marg finally answered. "It's because you don't know me at all, Heather. You've

been terribly self-absorbed these past years. People change. They grow up and sometimes they grow around things."

"You've grown around me, is that it?"

"I suppose so. I felt very hurt and jilted by you when we were steady pals. I never had the burning desire that you and Victoria had for adventure, but…"

"What, you're calling Boots 'Victoria' now? She hates that name."

"She uses it, it's on her card. Dr. Victoria Hatfield. She made it, Heather, all the way to a professional woman. Boots made it."

"Boots made it. I miss her." Heather sniffed. "She's not coming back. Lester is so proud."

"He's worried about you," Marg said.

"He needn't worry, I'm all right just like you're all right. What, are we going to be two old maids? You've got your parents, but I've got…"

"You've got us, Heather, all of us. Me, but you have to take me as I am, because that's who I've become. You have Clifford and Gert and Gus and certainly Lester; after all, he made something out of Boots."

For the first time in years, lifelong friends, sisters since childhood, laughed together.

Chapter 5

The Dance Floor

They reconnected that afternoon on the beach on Spensers Island, or at least Heather felt they did. Whether the experience was the same for Marg was an open question. Because once Heather opened up, she couldn't stop talking.

She told of the razzings, the tricks, the war, some but not much of what she witnessed at close range. She referred to but didn't go into detail about her first detention, how it happened and why. She skipped the events of a year and half later when another incident brought her up on charges that got her booted out of the Canadian Army.

Heather had no idea how long she had been talking. She was both exhausted and rejuvenated. She had come to fix Marg but had begun, she realized, to fix herself.

By the time Heather ran out of words, the tide was full, and they were forced to move to higher ground. They were turning back, walking along a path at the edge of the beach, when Marg said, "He was married."

She was opening up and Heather wanted her response to be emphatic and respectful. "You loved him, though, didn't you? Really loved him."

"Yes." Marg faltered and stopped. She turned her back to Heather. "Don't get involved with a married man," Marg cried over her shoulder in a voice that carried the pain of a thousand jilted lovers sharing their agony.

"I'm not," Heather said and wanted to add that she hated men more than loved them, if that was true. If that wasn't just all the junk of the past few years. She didn't know, but she told Marg the truth: She hadn't been on a date in three years. There was absolutely no man, no woman, nobody in her life. "I don't know, Marg, there are many things I need right now, and romance isn't one of them. I need to be able to understand myself, to lose the fears and misdirection I sometimes experience."

"He wasn't happy," Marg said, and Heather realized Marg hadn't heard what she'd said. It was Marg's turn again and Heather let her go.

"For all practical purposes his marriage had ended and was over long ago. He hung on until his children were out of the house."

There was silence for several seconds, then Heather asked, "He has grown children?"

"Yes, he's older, fifty-one to be exact."

More silence as they left the beach and reached Marg's front door.

"Cliff and Gert have gone to Parrsboro. Cliff likes the food at that new place, they go every Sunday. Come on in, I'll make us some tea."

Marg always referred to her parents by their first names, unusual perhaps, but many things are to people unaccustomed to uniqueness and individuality, two characteristics which thrive along this coast.

They sat in the kitchen, at the island Gert insisted Clifford make for her after she saw one in one of those fancy US magazines that cost twenty dollars. Gert had complained about the price as she forked over her money. She now had the only kitchen island in Spensers Island, as she liked to tell people.

After they were settled, Marg continued as if she hadn't stopped. Heather had been right: Marg, whether she admitted it or not, badly needed to unburden herself.

"It went on for almost four years, but in the end, he felt he couldn't leave his wife after all." Marg was trying to stay strong; only the tiniest single tear rolling beadlike down her oval cheek betrayed her situation.

Heather felt Marg's distress and it brought on slight tremors. The earth itself was spinning backwards, not just because of Marg or even Heather herself, but because of their vulnerability and pain. Marg had been let down by a man. Heather had been let down by her country's military.

Heather had felt fear up close; war is nothing like the movies. The smell of shit and blood, for one thing. Your skin frozen in that desert heat that bogs you down, constricting your movements. Now Marg was reaching out and Heather was failing to respond, less than two hours after she accused Marg of the same thing.

"We had plans," Marg continued as if talking to herself. Was she even aware Heather hadn't responded? "Crazy when I think of it now, but I was in love with him, you see, and that made the difference."

"I kicked a sergeant in the testicles," Heather blurted. A strange thing to say under the circumstances but it was at least, she thought, an offering of sorts. The abrupt statement brought the conversation to a halt, as Marg looked at Heather with an expression that suggested surprise and a touch of shock.

"You kicked a man?"

"Yes, he was bothering me, he claimed I was weak and would get them all killed. I got hauled up on charges."

"Was that in Afghanistan?"

"Yes. They said I was under stress, but what I was really under was constant sneering and a great deal of sexual harassment and innuendo."

Marg refilled their cups. It seemed it was Heather's turn to talk again.

"The official decision might be that I was unstable, I guess that's the word they'll use. I haven't got my medical discharge papers yet, but if they say I'm unstable or something like that it might impact other opportunities in the future." Heather stirred her coffee, Marg looking at her intently. "I mean, I have to do something with my life." She paused to take a sip, attempting to sound natural because her next question was difficult to ask and might cause an angry response. "I thought I'd ask you about teaching."

"You want to be a teacher now? After all this time, you want to teach?"

"I'm not sure about it, it was just a thought," Heather replied.

"Heather, to be a teacher, you must want to do it. Not just want. You must be dedicated to it. You decided long ago that wasn't your route."

"So you're saying I'm too late, is that it?"

"No, but being in the army, they'll probably want to look at your record. If it says something about erratic behavior, I don't know."

"It wasn't erratic. I kicked him with good reason, and I don't plan to be punished for it the rest of my life." Her tone suddenly had an edge to it, more like menace or threat than heartfelt confession and making her idea of being a schoolteacher seem, at that very second, totally unreasonable. Heather felt another avenue close.

Marg felt it too. She took Heather's hand and gently squeezed it. "Nobody is going to hold anything else against you. We just want you to get well and be happy."

It was Heather's turn to cry.

*

Heather was conflicted driving home. A rush of feelings overcame this ex-soldier in distress. At one point in the afternoon Marg had scoffed, "What were we doing in Afghanistan, anyway?"

"Helping people" was Heather's only reply. She couldn't begin to reveal or even explain in rational terms what she had seen there. The huge divergence in the culture between men who lived in the second century and young women desperate for a modern education.

Heather had unburdened herself and felt less anxiety, yet she was more perplexed about her future. If teaching wasn't suitable—and she was certain from the afternoon with Marg that it wasn't—then what?

"You can worry too much about yourself," Marg had said, and yes, it was entirely possible to worry too much. But it wasn't really worry; it was more dread of what her military papers would say. Heather felt she was adrift, untied from the wharf, drifting, bobbing as a piece of flotsam. There was just no place to anchor.

When she arrived at the Bar, Lester was beside himself.

"That damn fool got my boat hung up on the rocks again. He's off Spensers Island, wonder you didn't see him. I've told Gus time and again he's going to ruin my Cape Islander. Now he's going to have to stay there until midnight to get off."

Heather understood Lester was more worried about his son than his boat. The constant care sagged his shoulders at times. Yet he permitted Gus to take the boat out by himself because he wanted the boy to live a life. Down syndrome or not.

He stared straight ahead for a moment, then said, "How is Marg?"

"We had a good talk. How come you never told me about her romance?"

Lester straightened himself and ran his hands along his suspenders over his healthy girth. His glasses had grown thicker over the years, and his hair was half gray now. He was sixty-one, the type of man who naturally stooped passing under a doorway. A big, soft-spoken man.

"I don't know," he said. "It was never much talked about, you understand. Gert never mentioned it at all, and Cliff only did when she wasn't around. Truth be told, I didn't have much to tell you, except Marg was seeing a schoolteacher and he was older."

"And married," Heather replied.

"Yes, Cliff and Gert were worried, but Cliff didn't want to interfere, and Gert, of course, is a bull in a china shop. There's just the two of us for supper."

Lester had made lasagna, one of his specialties. As an accomplished chef he had many dishes, including a dozen different ways to cook chicken, the very best of which was outdoors in a hole in the ground wrapped in tinfoil and wet newspapers. The lasagna was already bubbling away in the wood stove and the aroma filled the float house.

"I levelled the dance floor this afternoon," Lester said, and Heather smiled.

"I can't believe you've kept it all these years," she replied, remembering the dances under the stars with a full tide and the moon on the water. What times. The floor had broken off from somebody's home that floated in the summer she was seven. Everything happened when she was seven. Her mother died, she came to live with Lester, the floor floated in, Cliff taught them how to dance. Boots already mostly knew, and she instructed too until Marg and Heather were proficient in the jive and waltz and Lester had demonstrated the foxtrot and whirled them all around the floor. Then there was the "boggy-woogy," a dance Boots made up herself.

The dance floor was a piece of good luck. The dances that year had been a diversion, and they were especially fun when you could get the old folks up. It was no problem with Lester, even Gus liked to waltz, but when Cliff and Gert took the floor, watch out; they could move to the tunes coming from the portable radio and knock you right off the floor onto the beach with a swing of Gertie's sharp hips or Cliff's elbows.

"Cliff is another Gordie Howe with those elbows," Lester remarked once, watching his brother-in-law sweep the floor, swirling his tall, lean wife of fifty years in his arms, looking as pleased as punch.

The dance floor was from a house broken up years ago. Apple River is at the end of one arm of the Bay of Fundy. The Fundy is the recipient of the powers of the universe, moving enough water twice a day to tilt the earth. Things, loosened by the tide or torn to pieces by storms, drift up the bay. Lobster traps, pieces of the fishery that refuse to sink, oil cans and parts of old boats, a barn door—once on the water they watched an outhouse float by, the little shack on its back, a third of it submerged. The half-moon cut in its door told them it was not a little storage shed. An array of material might go bobbing by at any time when you're coming up the Chignecto coast.

Dwellings that once belonged to a family, floors that once held the happy feet of children, claimed by the sea. Did those old houses ever hold the laughter of brothers and sisters? Were there prayers or profanity? Was there kindness or cruelty? Old houses have their stories to tell but leave much to the imagination.

Lester had a theory about the origins of their dance floor, that it was part of a house in Hopewell, New Brunswick, on the opposite shore. The family were fed up with things there and wanted to move across the water to Nova Scotia. They went across the sea ice too late in the season. The story, according to Lester, was that the bank had put a lien upon the house. So, the owners picked it up and moved. They left the horse barn but nothing else. It was late in the season, but they thought it had been cold enough and they were desperate. Halfway across, the ice gave way under the weight, and they lost the house and three horses.

"I hope that isn't where our dance floor came from," Heather said upon first hearing that story. "It sounds like one of Cliff's tall tales." She never wanted to believe that story, as she always loved horses.

Gus told her that many houses fall into the sea. Lester elaborated, "Where the land is soft soil, the natural seawall has depleted, gobbled up by rolling waves pushed by rising water. Higher spring tides take great chunks from the coastal cliffs, a withdrawal never compensated for. The sea takes what it wants, and the land is loosened by frozen water seeping into crevices and wedging into cracks the human eye can't see. But the cracks are there and so is the water, always expanding."

Gert would say that's what she wasn't going to do, get old and fall into the sea. Then that cackle would go up and everybody would laugh or at least smirk except Marg, who'd have a pleading expression, as if saying, "Okay, Mother, you can stop now."

Those who lived along the coast knew the truth, that what falls into the sea often travels or is pushed up the bay, and what comes up the bay, often as not, stays. The wreck of a Cape Islander is a prime example. It washed into Horseshoe Cove ten years ago and remains a rotted hulk that provides a shelter for kayakers and hikers.

It is understood that whatever can be salvaged is taken.

Lester had hauled the old floor out of the tide, again with a borrowed tractor. He let it dry out away from the water. He planned to cut it up for firewood, but the children started playing on it and then dancing on it when Gus brought down his portable radio that first night and they were under the stars. Heather's mother came down, guided on Lester's arm. She was wrapped in a white blanket, and the bright moon cast a silvery glow over her. Her blond hair appeared snow white. She was both drawn and beautiful as she smiled at Heather. That minute in the moonlight was how Heather remembered her mother. A cherished childhood image, one of many in that last summer with her. Marg and her parents, Boots, Lester, and Gus too, in fact the floor itself, were all part of something Heather cherished.

The floor had survived hurricanes and big tides that moved it, tossed it about, sweeping a ton of water a minute over it, pushing the floor at times down the Bar, turning it around and around like a playing card, but through it all the floor stayed on the Bar as if it had a purpose there, a useful purpose. That's how Heather felt about it.

Chapter 6

Hung Up with Angus

It was almost midnight, threatening rain, and the boat was rocking back and forth, still caught up in seaweed-covered rocks, the first outcropping of old coastal cliffs that had been worn away over thousands of years. They were close to shore, and Gus had the resources to yell for someone to call his father, tell him he was hung up, not to worry. Such messages are respected and passed along the coast.

The tide was lifting the hull slowly, rocking it back and forth a little more firmly now. There was no moon, the water was inky and angry, slapping the bow with a wet fist, splattering Gus, squeezing his face. He tried to shake off the residue, but already the salt was in his mouth. The wind was spitting at him. He was cold and hungry. He hadn't bothered to bring anything to eat, as he'd only been going out for a tide. His coffee thermos was empty hours ago.

Angus was asleep, but Gus would have to wake him soon just in case he needed a little more muscle to pry 'er off the rock. Also, Gus wasn't a good drinker. He knew he wasn't supposed to drink. It conflicted with his meds, but he drank anyway. He had been ill and still woozy. They had polished off a pint between them. Angus always drank the most. He said he had a reputation to uphold. Gus poured most of his into the sea, but not enough. He had thrown up the rest of it.

Making everything worse, as he sat there shivering, Gus knew his father was upset with him over the boat and his carelessness and for hanging around with Angus, whom Lester heartily disliked. Gus reasoned he was old enough to pick his own friends, and in truth, Angus was his only friend. That was the truth of it: Gus felt safe and sheltered with his family.

Angus was a man with a wasted existence, according to most people. He lacked money, family, and friends. Except for Gus.

How's that for a shitty life? Angus was an outcast in the community. He was blamed for things, mostly for stealing lobster, never proven but often mentioned.

"He's wasted his life. You hang out with him and where do you think you're going to end up?" Lester had asked his son once, immediately realizing the meaninglessness of his remark. Gus wasn't going anywhere. He was and always would be Lester's responsibility. His son was different; people often shied away from Gus. Lester had seen it himself. He didn't approve of Angus, but he understood too. He had promised his wife, "God in Heaven, dearest, I will look after him, always." His last words to her. Gus would always be cared for, not in an institutional home somewhere but here, with him. Lester had promised.

Gus was twelve years old the first time he saw Heather with her mother, that first summer with the dance floor. He couldn't take his eyes off her, she was so different from Boots and Marg, so white, so bright, like a star or something. Gus tried to walk around to study her from every direction. It was after that he and his father had some serious discussions. That summer was the best year of Gus's life. He had gained a beautiful sister, and she was living with them. Part of his talk with his father was about sisters and brothers and what was and what wasn't. Gus was always part of the gang. The girls never excluded him from their activities or games. If they were doing something Gus considered too girly, he'd walk down the Bar and tend his trapline. The gang included his sister, Boots, his cousin Marg and her parents, and his brand new sister Heather. Outside his immediate circle there was Angus. No one else.

Heather's mother, Gus's aunt, had been really sick. They were blond, Heather was like her mother. Over the years Gus watched her grow, taller than Boots, but never as big boned. Boots, people said, looked like Lester in a dress.

The tricky coastal wind was up in a new direction, suddenly coming up the bay. The Cape Islander swayed, bucked once, and broke free. Gus hit the motor, and they were clear of the rock but facing into a stiff wind. It was a cold, miserable voyage up the coast to Apple River. Angus was coughing as he staggered off at Lester's homemade dock inside Apple

River Bay. He grunted, "Night," and weaved his way up the beach and off into the woods to a cabin somewhere.

Gus felt sorry for Angus. Even now, when Dad was mad at him, Gus felt secure. He had people. Angus had nobody, and it always made Gus sad when he watched his only friend walk into the dark woods by himself.

*

Despite the fact he drank too much, Angus had good night vision. He knew where he was going. He had walked this path for years. He was always able to navigate on the water too. Even at night when the bay was blocked with fog, leaving many more claustrophobic than scared, Angus could find his way up the bay and around Apple River Bar when the tide was running. He loved the bay at night. If the water was placid, he heard sounds carried across the surface from both the New Brunswick and Nova Scotia coasts. After years he still heard sounds and noises he couldn't identify. A squawk or squeal on the surface of the water. Angus was never scared of such things. He almost welcomed them, as if they offered a lonely man some comfort. He liked the bay, being out on the water, at night, and that's what got him in trouble in the first place. They searched his boat and found half a dozen lobsters that Angus had caught himself. He had a couple of illegal traps, he confessed. His neighbours weren't having it, they threw them back in the water. "When you steal a lobster, you steal from us. Those that paid for licenses. Those of us who paid for boats and gear."

They cuffed him hard and took his gasoline and emptied his tank into the bay. He drifted ashore an hour later. That type of episode happened more than once.

Angus often wondered how his life went off the tracks. When he got a little older, he tried to put his early life into some organized mental picture. There were a series of dads, Mom's boyfriends. Some were nice to him, some weren't, but none of them were in his life for very long. The good ones ignored him, and he liked that the best. His mother's name was Ruth, but most of her boyfriends called her Skinny. For a good time, call Skinny, they used to say, or one of them said, because it stuck in Angus's mind. His mom died of alcohol poisoning. The boyfriends were gone, none having made a permanent bond with Angus.

He had tried marriage, but at eighteen and his bride a year younger, neither knew enough about each other, about life or love or much of anything else. He was divorced at twenty-two and joined the army. Two years later he was given a medical discharge when he managed to blow off his thumb. A small pension let him buy a piece of land nobody wanted. He lived in a lean-to until he built his hobbit-hole-like cabin.

Angus knew he was an outcast. He knew Lester didn't like him and he knew Lester liked almost everybody. That pinched his tortured heart in some manner. He didn't exactly understand what made him morose or why he was a social pariah. He had never lifted a finger against any man or woman.

*

Lester was sitting at the kitchen table playing solitaire when Gus walked in. The kitchen clock said twenty minutes to three. Gus's hair, the sandy shade of his mother's, clung to his forehead. He was cold and wet. Lester looked at him for only a second.

"You all right?" Lester asked.

"Yeah."

"You know you're not supposed to catch cold, and look at you. You take your medicine?"

"Yes, I'm fine."

"Boat all right?'

"Yeah, we glided right off there."

"So, I'm not going to see any dents or damage to the hull?"

"No, you won't."

"Well, all right then, I'm going to bed. There's lasagna in the warming oven I wrapped up for you."

"Thanks."

As he turned to go upstairs, Lester said, "What were you doing in there, anyway? I told you to stay out of there."

"There's a halibut hole in there, we was hoping to hook one as the tide dropped." Gus couldn't look at his father. He felt the way he did years ago when he was sixteen and brought home a letter from the principal informing Lester that Gus had failed grade six again. Lester had read the letter slowly, folded it up, and put it back in the envelope.

"All right then," he'd said, getting up from the table. "You don't have to go back."

They were the most powerful words Gus had ever heard. It was the end of the taunts, and the growing sting each year of being the oldest pupil in the room. Not going back broke the shackles of torment in his young life. Gus walked outside that day after those powerful words from his father. He didn't walk down to the Bar; he would never do what he knew he was about to do on magical ground, it was a sacred place. No, on that day of freedom Gus had walked the other way, across watery sand where the tide had left Apple River Bay a wet marsh. He went up the open beach of Chignecto along the sloping bank of crab grass escaping buff-coloured soil. Coastal cliffs are smaller here but rise higher as they proceed towards the open Bay of Fundy.

Gus had walked a mile down the coast until he found a secluded place where he could climb the bank in the woods above the water. Surrounded by thick evergreens of various species, Gus sat down and cried like a baby. He was grown, man sized, a coward and a sissy, but he didn't have to hear those names anymore. Names they called him when he wouldn't fight. No more names was good, but every happiness has its price: He was so ashamed of himself for crying like a baby he cried harder, finally making himself sick. Then Gus had wiped his face off with the back of his hand, which he dried on the seat of his pants, and went home. He was free.

Lester never spoke of school again and neither did Gus. His sister went to college and veterinary school. Gus stayed home with his father.

There were times over the years when Gus wondered about Heather's father. No one had ever seen him, except Heather's mother of course. Lester never said much except his sister had a one-night stand as she called it and never a bit ashamed or anything like that. No, proud as punch at having a baby.

Gert wanted the child, but Heather was given to Lester's care. That was her mother's doing.

Her mother never really talked about Heather's father because she knew nothing about him. Heather's mother described herself as a "free spirit." For some reason Lester said that pretty well described her. They were close, Heather's mom two years younger than Lester. He was always protecting her, pulling her out of bad places, looking after her, lending her money when she was broke. So naturally, where would she go when she was dying and had a child to care for? Since that time Heather had spent her life with Lester. Winters in Advocate Harbour in a snug two-storey house by the road, and summers here at the Bar, in a hollow old dwelling that Lester had salvaged, claiming squatter's rights on property that wasn't his.

"It's temporary," he said the first few years, but that was a couple of decades ago.

For some reason Gus was thinking of those memories as he ate the lasagna. He was weary from his night on the water. Then he put his head down and fell asleep at the kitchen table, where his father found him the next morning at ten past six. Lester looked at his son and felt a small pang in his heart. *Dear God, what will happen to that boy when I'm gone?* He thought he should lose some weight; Boots didn't need him, but Gus did. *Gus always will.* And Heather, he had to get her straight too. Always lots to do. He roused Gus and sent him upstairs to bed and made a coffee. Then he went outside to greet the day.

The breeze was surprisingly warm for so early in the morning. The radio said it was the warmest May on record. The midnight rolling tide that had washed Gus off the rocks had receded. A lone osprey glided silently over the empty basin, the bird low, wings spread wide in an easy glide, eyes on the prize just in case Mother Nature might leave a morsel behind.

Lester, coffee in hand, walked down the beach to inspect his Cape Islander. At low tide he could walk around the hull and have a good look. Then maybe when the tide was back he might run her down the coast for a bit for flounder.

Lester watched the osprey make a long swoop and come gliding back again. Was it really hunting or just flying for the fun of it? He walked up under his boat resting on the empty beach. He knew there would be some damage, and of course there was. A few new gouges in a twelve-year-old wooden boat wouldn't matter to most people, but Lester's boat was the *Dory Anne*, named after his late wife. He could have restricted Gus's use of his boat, but that would be like denying the lad a bit of his mother. Lester couldn't do that.

Heather was in the kitchen getting coffee when Lester came back, and she joined him on the little porch that Gus had put together. It had a rather haphazard appearance, but Lester said it wasn't any more off balance than most people he knew around here, and Gus was proud of it, so he didn't complain. Besides, as Gert pointed out, it went with the lopsided look of the float house with its driftwood exterior, rather artfully replacing the lost backside. Cliff had built on the second storey in the third year when Lester held a ceremony and claimed the salvage rights, as if there was anyone to dispute it. It was a good party.

"Tide will be in at midafternoon. Could be a fine day, want to go for some flounder for supper?"

"Sure," Heather replied. "Gus coming with us?"

Lester heaved a sigh. "I suppose so, he hasn't much else to do, has he?"

Heather put her hand on Lester's shoulder and squeezed lightly. "Gus is doing the best he can. I know you want him to have a full-time job, but that's hard for him."

"He's had jobs, works hard, but can't learn. He'll be at the park this summer, cleaning the grounds, clearing brush, things like that. He doesn't mind it. He goes along at his own pace He worked with Clifford a bit but couldn't cut a board right, couldn't measure."

"I told you before you could get a disability pension for him."

"I don't need a pension for him. I sold my big boat and gear, I've got enough to support him without going hat in hand to the government, enough people are doing that."

"So, we'll go out about midafternoon?" Heather said, seeing the pension discussion was ending as it always did.

"Yeah, around three should be good. You want some scrambled eggs and bacon?"

"Sure, but give yourself another coffee, I'm going to do one of my favourite things in the early morning, walk down the Bar. Looks like a fine day."

She pulled a sweater around her shoulders and headed to the beach. Lester watched, thinking how much she looked like her mother and how different her mother was from his other sister, Gert, a good soul even if you wanted to occasionally strangle her.

Gert had told him once after Doherty died that if something happened to him, she and Clifford would take in Gus. But that was a long time ago; Gert was over seventy now and wouldn't be taking in anybody. Lester decided he had to live long enough to see Gus through life. That might be a tall order.

The osprey had disappeared down the waterless gorge that is Apple River Bay at low tide.

Chapter 7

The Rescue

Lester brought egg sandwiches, a large thermos of coffee, and fuel. At three o'clock they were heading out of Apple River Bay into the wider Chignecto Bay.

Gus had slept until it was time to go and was still groggy and tired. Lester made him have a bath, because he stank, and Gus didn't argue because he knew he did. Lester's final instruction was that Gus take off that new shirt Lester just bought him two weeks ago at Mansour's in Amherst and wear his oilskins. By the end of a fishing trip Gus was bound to be wearing fish guts, flounder blood, and specks of various unknown marine residues.

They were going up the coast just past Halibut Head and into Spicer's Cove. They knew where to fish, and if the winds were calm enough, they would handline for what was known as *filet au sole* in the finer restaurants of New York where it isn't caught, but in the country where it is harvested, its name is flounder, and way down home, it's simply called flat fish.

There are many types of water and various kinds of winds. The gentle breezes of a sheltered harbour are nothing like what might come up in a big body of water like the Bay of Fundy, which is connected to another bay called the Gulf of Maine, which leads to a vast body of water known as the Atlantic Ocean. There are miles upon miles of cliffs along these coastal waterways. Natural wind tunnels if the conditions are right. Old sailors talk of facing a williwaw, a banshee howling blow out of the nor' east, and the temperature drops faster than the slamming of an outhouse door.

You can't escape the wind on the coast, but they were experienced, knew enough to stay close to the cliffs, where there was some shelter. Gus already had the hooks baited and his handline in the water. He watched the baited hooks, dragged down by lead weights, disappear into the depths.

"There should be a prize for first flounder," he said excitedly, and then realized he sounded childlike and said nothing more.

Hungry herring gulls kept their eyes on them. The birds know by nature where the food supply is hiding. The gulls squawked while sweeping easily past in a wing-wide glide, waiting for throwback. Their boat bobbed in the water, twenty feet off the cliff. There was an underwater gully here that ran deep and often held a good supply of flounder.

They settled in with three lines with double hooks in the water as the usual ocean garbage drifted by. The worst were the plastic tags used in the lobster industry.

"They put a man on the moon," Lester said, "but can't figure out a substitute for plastic on a lobster trap."

Sometimes Heather fished out pieces of gear, the remains of an old lobster trap, even old rope. She watched as orange and green lines danced by in a frantic entanglement. More plastic tags, like white butterflies, dancing on the wavering surface. An entangled piece of net drifted by. People who use the ocean most have the most responsibility, but they leave it dirty.

Lester had one hand on his line, halfheartedly fishing while his binoculars were scanning two other boats nearby.

"I *thought* that was Cliff out there." He waved, and Cliff gave him a big, "Ahoy!"

Heather heard Gus declared excitedly, "I think I got one."

"Too fast, too fast, you haven't had enough time to catch anything," Lester replied.

"Oh yeah?" Gus was going hand over hand bringing up his line as fast as possible until he saw the hooks still carried the chunks of white sand shark meat. Quietly he let the line sink back to the bottom. Five minutes later Cliff's boat had its engine not only running but roaring towards them.

Cliff had a ship-to-shore radio in his boat; Lester didn't. Cliff cut the engine, quickly pulling neatly alongside, making enough wake to rock both boats. Before he spoke they understood something was wrong. The big face of Cliff the joker carried a very serious expression. "There's a freighter in trouble right off Isle Haute," he said breathlessly. "They need help, I'm going out."

Lester has the glasses to his eyes again. "Where are they?"

"Just off the north tip, you can only see the bow. It's sticking out behind the island."

Both boats were suddenly tearing through the water into the open bay. Heather and Gus hardly had time to pull up their lines before Lester was running fast almost alongside Cliff at full speed. The air turned cold in the open bay. The water was rough, billowy whitecaps fiercely slapping fast-moving hulls. Nobody noticed; all parties were looking ahead to the island that stood almost in the middle of the Bay of Fundy.

They were miles away from the three-hectare Isle Haute, but it was easily seen from both sides of Fundy. Its hundred-foot cliffs stand out as a great fortress near the mouth of the Minas Basin. The afternoon was bright, and between the haze on the distant horizon and the glare off the water was the dark bow of an oceangoing ship with angry, curling smoke rising in a rolling plume.

"She's run aground, maybe," Lester said, mainly to himself as there was nothing but the roar of wind and the noise of engines and plowing water, destroyers of human words. Then, "Something's coming around the island!" he yelled, pointing with his glasses in hand. They were hitting the waves hard as if the water were a firmer substance. After the bow bump came the trough, plunging the boat downward, drilling it into the ocean, only to be pulled up and sacked again. The ride was rough, the noise a cocktail of machine and nature accompanied by the hollow slap of wooden hulls on pitching, undulating seawater.

"I think it's a lifeboat. It's full of people," Lester yelled, and somehow Cliff heard and shook his head.

The white speck was around the island and in full view now. A power launch, a fourteen-foot wooden lifeboat. It was crowded. Heather counted a dozen heads and maybe more, too far yet to tell if they were men, women, or children.

Everybody was suddenly working, Cliff and Lester at full speed as Heather was already standing on the gunnel of Lester's boat waiting for the right turn, the right wave to jump onto Cliff's Cape Islander, which was slightly faster and would reach the men first. She had the first aid kit and bandages stuffed under her heavy sweater. She timed it perfectly and made a good jump, and dear god, didn't—without warning—didn't Gus follow her with a look of complete triumph when he landed hard next to her on Cliff's slippery and bouncing deck. Heather was already ripping bandages and checking the first aid kit.

The problem was being heard, so hand signals had to do. The wind was coming up the bay, blowing right at them, rising to a good clip. There were a dozen men in the lifeboat, some with the frozen faces of cadavers. They were wide-eyed and gesticulating as Cliff cut his engine and swirled in close. There were more. Sprawled across three laps was a young man with trousers full of blood. Other laps contained an older sailor in an officer's uniform. He was middle aged, unconscious, with his head lolling port side. Heather knew he was dead.

Suddenly a lot of chatter arose from the lifeboat. She realized for the first time these men were foreign. Some of them weren't speaking English. Cliff lashed the two boats together so he could as gently as possible place the injured men on his deck, taking them one at a time in his big arms as if he were lifting sleeping children. The boats were bobbing as Heather focused on the younger man in bloody trousers. She yelled at Cliff to cut open the man's pants quickly. On Heather's instruction he unbuckled the sailor's belt and ripped down his trousers with one clean jerk.

Heather went to his aid. He was lying on his back, bleeding profusely from a wound in his groin which someone had tried to control by pressing on it with a rag. She immediately realized his femoral artery had been damaged and the man would bleed out unless she could stop it. It was much too high up the leg for a tourniquet: She would have to cut into his groin and clamp the artery. She had seen this before in Afghanistan and remembered some of what the medic had said not to her, of course, because she was a woman and should have been back home knitting, but to another, male, soldier.

She got out a scalpel and made a long vertical cut extending on both ends of the bleeding area. It wasn't easy in a rocking boat on a man who wouldn't lie still and in unstable, fluctuating light. She remembered the medic's advice: "You have to press harder than you think to get through the skin. Incisions heal from side to side, not end to end. The important thing is to make it long enough so you can see what you're doing." But there was too much blood to see anything. She had to feel the pulsating artery. At least the blood was warm. Otherwise, her fingers might have been too cold to feel anything. The seaman cursed and wriggled as she cut him down to just above the artery and pushed a closed pair of pointed scissors either side of it, forced them open to free it and then, entirely by feel, clamped it with the largest pair of artery forceps in the kit. She knew it would have been better to use proper padded forceps and what she was doing would damage the artery and make it more difficult for the definitive surgery he would need if he survived to get to hospital. Still, like the army medic said, her job was to keep him alive. She tacked the skin edges together with three stitches and kept pressing on them until the flow of blood got weaker and then stopped. His heart had failed! She started to rhythmically push down on his chest to try and restore a bit of circulation. "Don't you fucking die on me. I'm not going to give up and you won't either." At least it was cold, which would have given him a better chance. She soon became exhausted, so she got Gus to take over while she went back to the major wound. She heard and felt a rib break, but Heather shouted to Gus to carry on. The three boats were bobbing side by side, the Norwegians stunned, their boat still overcrowded. Cliff and Lester offered to take the sailors off the lifeboat, but either they couldn't get the idea across, or the Norwegians wanted to stay together. Occasionally one or two would look back at their abandoned ship, but there was little to see. Most of them watched Heather work on the sailor with urgent intensity. Cliff smiled broadly, which was rather incongruous with the deadly white, silent body of one of the men on his deck and the occasional whimpering from the unconscious man Heather was helping.

"Military training," Cliff yelled loudly at the Norwegians, pointing at Heather, and the Norwegians all nodded in perfect unison as if they had practiced it. Cliff said later he thought of the bobbing heads in the back windows of vehicles. It was no joke at the time, he confessed. The crew nodded silently and earnestly; most understood him, some appeared not to, while a few repeated the word. Maybe they all did; Cliff wasn't certain.

It was only revealed later that there was such apathy among the sailors because they were leaderless. The captain and first mate were dead. The first mate on Cliff's deck, the captain unaccounted for.

Cliff had immediately radioed the news of the crew to the coast guard. He noticed there were now two lobster boats approaching the burning freighter from the other side of the bay. From what Lester could see the freighter was an old European ship, probably steam powered. If she was sinking, which they didn't always do, and cold seawater was running into the engine room and hit hot boilers, the boilers would explode. Cliff was already warning the lobstermen on the radio that they should stay clear. Salvage was not worth dying over.

The Norwegians started talking among themselves. They let their eyes leave Heather and return to the lobster boats almost to Isle Haute. It was more difficult to make out as they were all suddenly moving in the opposite direction, heading for shore at top speed. A party of three boats, Clifford with the biggest engine, powered ahead with Lester and the Norwegians running behind.

Gus had the sailor breathing but appeared ill himself. At first, he had been upset and paralyzed by the sight of all the blood. He overcame his fear when Heather told him to scramble down below deck and grab blankets and pillows off the bunks.

It was full speed ahead for Advocate Harbour. The wake rocked the boats like a carnival ride with a frigid spray covering everything. Twenty minutes from shore a helicopter flew overhead. Cliff yelled to everyone it was from the Canadian military base, Greenwood, across the bay. If anyone heard, no one answered. They were relieved that medical aid would be there before them.

Heather was losing feeling in her fingers. The injured man slightly moved occasionally, letting the outside world know of his suffering with a low moan. He was much younger than the dead man next to him, and physically fit. She would not let him die. For reasons she did not understand, she knew it was her mission to save him. She talked to him over the uproar of wind and water. Words he could never hear. She did it anyway, ordered him to stay alive and fight for his life. She must save him to…what? Save herself?

Twenty-five minutes from shore he attempted to move once, to somehow adjust himself unconsciously. Lester and Cliff were yelling something back and forth, but she couldn't catch more than a word or two before the wind snatched the rest away. Her back was paralyzed from her position, sprawled wide legged across the man's knees, him face down on the deck, with both her hands frozen on the sailor's leg, his blood already drying on her hands. Both Cape Islanders were wide open, and a fine wake covered her. The saltwater stung her eyes, nettled her skin as if she were attacked by a nest of angry insects. She had placed one pillow beneath her knees, which were taking a beating as the deck was in constant motion, hitting the waves full force. She encouraged Gus to help and after much resistance Gus finally did what she requested. Maybe there was the look of pleading in her eyes, but when Gus lifted the sailor's head it was done with gentleness. Gus's hands were slightly shaking as he placed the pillow under the injured man.

The wharf in Advocate Harbour was in the centre of the village. The arrival of a helicopter had brought out the local citizenry. A helicopter was always bad news. Someone was seriously hurt and needed to be airlifted. There is a closeness in a small coastal community where *neighbour* is more than a word. What hurts one harms all. An ambulance from Parrsboro arrived just as Cliff was docking. Heather couldn't let go of the sailor's wound in case the bleeding would get worse. In exasperation she looked up at faces leaning over the wharf, staring back at her, even taking pictures. She told Cliff, first thing, to put a blanket over the dead sailor. Heather was still on her knees. Her back was throbbing, her hands numb, and her fingers were not working well. She could hear the whirl and click of cameras. As Cliff tied up, Heather heard footsteps coming down the ladder. She was more than ready for relief when the paramedics were by her side.

"We'll take it from here." They quickly examined the deep gash while putting a needle in his arm. Somehow two medics turned him over and began chest compressions. Blood from a plastic bag flowed into the wounded man. There was a clatter on the wharf as more people arrived. While all this was going on Heather suddenly felt faint. She told the medevac crew what she had done.

"That's amazing," the leader said. "How on earth could you do that in a small rocking boat? I don't think I could have done it."

The injured man was still alive. Occasionally he stirred. "Thank God you're still alive," Heather said to him, getting to her feet as the medics lifted the sailor on a stretcher. Her ordeal was over, or so she thought.

She and Gus hugged each other. They would never forget that afternoon. One of the medics continued, "No matter what happens in the rest of your life, you'll always be the woman who saved a man's life.

Nothing anybody says or does to you can take that away. You should be very proud of yourself."

Those few words created a warmth in Heather. She had completed her mission. If the man lived, she would have done something worthy. For the first time in months, she felt accomplishment.

Her legs were so cramped Cliff had to help her. There was a warming bag for her hands and Cliff guided her around the deck to get her circulation back.

The wharf was crowded and noisy by then. The muffled hum of adults, the chatter of children, and barking dogs sniffing the excitement. And the whirl and click of cameras. But when the Norwegians arrived, their grim silence on the water dissolved immediately into an enthusiastic desire to shake the hand of every citizen of Cumberland County.

"They want you on the wharf," Cliff said, guiding her to the ladder.

"Who does?" Heather asked, her legs throbbing and wobbling, her back aching. Blood was on her hands and hair.

"The Norwegians, they're excited."

When Heather came topside, the sailors lined up to kiss her cheek and hug her. She was embarrassed by her appearance, not given time to clean herself up, and people were taking pictures. She felt one pair of arms around her after another. Most of the Norwegians spoke English, and the words *thank you* were whispered into her ears many times.

She wished people would stop taking pictures. Some had video cameras. There was no stopping the Norwegians now. They were all talking and shivering, despite the sun. Folks rushed to their vehicles to scoot Fido off his blanket for the needy sailors. They would be taken to a church hall to be fed. Planning was well underway, the helicopter was lifting off.

It took hours for the crowd to disperse. Heather was congratulated a hundred times. Cliff and Lester captivated clusters of onlookers with their firsthand accounts. Finally, when the ordeal was down to two dozen lingerers, Heather, Cliff, and Lester bade them goodbye. They motored up the coast, already missing the tide into Apple River Bay. They would spend the night with Cliff and Gert, taking the morning tide to the Bar.

Heather knew Lester was proud of her. He didn't comment often but showed it in other ways. You had to look to see it. His pride was obvious in his eyes. She knew his moods and particularly his jauntiness, the additional lightness in his step.

Gus bitterly complained they hadn't caught one single flounder.

Chapter 8

News Coverage

When they tied up in Spensers Island, Lester couldn't conceal his feeling; the pride was spilling out of him as if he were a leaky container.

"I was so proud of you today, Heather, the way you took over. That man would have died without you. I didn't know you were a nurse, you never said."

"I'm not, but I took a medical tech's course in the military and used it in Afghanistan, more than once."

"You don't need to think about that," he said, and she wondered if there was enough time right now, before they reached Cliff's front door, to make Lester understand it wasn't the blood and gore of war that had sent her packing. It was the fact she had followed her mother's example and never shied away from the truth, and it had cost her dearly. She had been back a month, and it was time he understood.

She began, "Maybe we should talk about it, because, dear uncle, you might have the wrong impression about things. The war was mostly boring. Hot, dry, and boring. The actual fighting was awful, and it impacted me because we were in the thick of it. But here's the thing, it wasn't just me. It impacted every soldier in our unit. They don't care for the term shell-shocked anymore, they've softened the term, but that's what it felt like to all of us. The shaking after, the nervous trembles, your bowels ready to let loose. They even have a name for it, the post-shootout shuffle."

Lester was watching as they walked through the row of Scotch pines into Cliff and Gert's front yard. Heather wished she had dragged him down the beach. Never enough time to explain things properly.

"It wasn't the war and gore. It was the men with me and the men over me. That's what wounded me in battle."

Lester looked wounded himself as Cliff opened the door with a glass of rum in his hand. The only subject tonight would be the past hours, the exciting aftermath of the day. It was riding high in Cliff's complexion. He had been answering questions with cameras and video held close to him, as if it was a news conference.

When they entered the kitchen, the room that made Gert's house look like a pregnant lighthouse, Gus, who had gone ahead of them, was excitedly telling his version of the day's adventure.

"There was blood everywhere," said Gus, using his fleshy arms to encompass everything.

Cliff poured drinks from a flask on the table. Gert was drinking white wine and looked unhappy. There was no sign of Marg or food.

"Well, here's the hero of the day." Gert jumped up and hugged Heather while Gus continued his story.

Cliff looked proud of himself, as he had already revealed the exciting happenings to his wife, but Gert wanted Heather's and Lester's versions too.

"Cliff always leaves things out, and then later, like two weeks later, he remembers to tell me a pertinent detail. How can you rely on a person like that?" Gert huffed, while looking rather admiringly at her husband. It had been her husband's boat that brought in the wounded, they were at the centre of things, and it was something to remember for later telling.

Not to her grandchildren, because there were not going to be any. Gert blamed everybody else.

She had produced an offspring, done her part; where were the rest of them? Marg would be thirty in a couple of years and wasn't even in a relationship. Still, for posterity, family stories matter, and by God, Gert was going to have every morsel, every detail of all of it. She couldn't wait any longer.

"So Heather, you're not a nurse, Cliff says, but you saved that sailor's life. Was that what you learned in the military or simple first aid they teach in Girl Scouts?"

The question infuriated Heather. She was hungry and tired and hated the flippancy of it, the manner in which Gert tried to level things to her viewpoint. "Girl Scouts?" Heather sniffed, hoping she sounded as dismissive as she felt. "There's no Girl Scouts on the shore that I know of, and first aid is never simple."

She left it at that. A silence filled the room to the point where even Gus stopped eating and looked at them all. Heather couldn't help herself. She hated the way Gert kept probing at her, and it brought back memories of other lives saved and lost in the field of combat, memories that were like lifting a tender scab, tearing it just enough to feel pain.

"Maybe you should be a nurse," Gert said, oblivious to any discomfort she was causing. Lester was more attuned to the atmosphere and changed the subject.

"Let's turn on the radio, get some music," Gus said, but it was a news bulletin they got, a fifteen-second flash from a US station about a rescue in the North Atlantic and the words "Norwegian crew."

"Is that us? What, didn't they say Norwegian?" Cliff asked.

Except Gert, they were all groggy and weren't certain what they had heard, but the last words really did sound like "Norwegian crew." There were no details, and they weren't in the North Atlantic. But a rescue of Norwegians. Could there be two seagoing disasters? If so, it was a bad day for Norwegian shipping.

A pall fell over them brought on by exhaustion. Only Gert was wired. She served lemon meringue pie and coaxed them to stay up for the news at ten o'clock, just to see what was going on.

Heather had another piece of pie. Gert made coffee, saying Marg was in Halifax again. Gus was asleep, and Lester and Cliff were groggy.

"That's what I do," Gert wheezed, "stay home and cook all day and you folks out there on the water having the time of your life."

That brought a chorus of jeers from the tired group, they were played out and Gert looked pleased with herself. They slumbered, most of the adventure seekers as Gert called them. At two minutes to ten she roused the sleepers and turned on the television. It was time for the national news.

They were still half asleep but stunned immediately when the news began.

"That's our boat," Gert shrieked, and there was Cliff docking his Cape Islander and there was Heather on her knees, blond hair slightly bloody and askew. There was another shot of her coming up the ladder to the wharf, flushed and golden, then in full sunlight, bloody and beautiful, but her heart sank as she was identified as "the soldier who saved a sailor's life." Then they plunged into the heart of the story with Cliff's big face on the screen. Shocked astonishment came over the group as they listened to the report. Then Gert continued her throaty gasps. There was Lester with a broad smile filling up the screen. His words were lost to Heather, as she felt herself slowly sinking in her chair.

They would find her out. Eventually know about her military experience. She didn't want to be called a hero only to be called a phony later. She couldn't afford to be labelled a hero, not with a less-than-honourable discharge hanging over her head. Already her world was changing, her life about to veer off into an unexpected course. A route she had never planned to travel.

They heard Marg's car arriving home from Halifax. Marg was startled to see them all spread around the room, trying to stay awake. She came into the group just in time to pick up the first ring of the telephone. A call from the Halifax newspaper.

"Yes, this is his house, do you want to speak to him?"

A hush fell over them as Cliff, rather unsteadily, weaved his way to the phone. They listened to one side of a conversation, except Cliff was giving a lot of yes and no answers, and once, "Yes, yes, that's right, my boat. It's called *The Gerty G.*" More listening, then, "Yes Heather is right here, I'll let you speak to her."

After the second network newscast at eleven o'clock, which was essentially the same, they were by then too worked up to sleep, and talk returned to tomorrow's interviews. Every journalist in the province was about to descend on them.

"Certainly not me, I wasn't there," declared Gert rather breathlessly, tightly crossing her thin legs and holding her wine glass at a distinct angle. She resembled an aging movie star from the 1930s. "Of course," she added, "I could give them a good description of the people who live here. You know, local colour, from here to Parrsboro."

"I'm the local storyteller," Cliff, fortified with drink, reminded her. "You're the chef and in charge of ambiance."

Gert looked at her husband sternly. If he weren't a hero, if that big face hadn't been plastered on television sets right across the country, she might give him a cuff, just for fun. The way they used to play. Instead, she was rolling around the word *ambiance*, trying to put the right fix on all of its meanings.

Cliff and Lester were singing then, their baritone voices giving a good rendition of "I'll Take You Home Again Kathleen" while a series of small yawns escaped the rest of them. Heather had fallen asleep in her chair; Marg, tired from the drive, was trying also to stay awake. When they finished singing, Lester yawned, sagging a bit to starboard. Soon his head slightly reclined. His mouth was just agape enough for everyone else to detect the soft purring, building to a good snore.

Gert sat. Marg made tea and wished she'd stayed in Halifax. She was so out of the loop on this big adventure, but so very proud of her Dad. She realized this was a day he would never forget. He had saved people. And she had missed it all.

Only Gert was wide awake. From Gert's perch at her island of pine and ceramic she looked over her family as if taking inventory. By midnight Heather was curled in a tight ball, Lester was asleep in the opposite corner, Cliff was chattering away to his daughter, who kept up a query of intelligent questions. Some, most, he couldn't answer. Gert accepted tea as the white wine was depleted. But what an evening.

*

"You're the star of the show, sweetheart," Gert said in the morning as Heather tried to back out of the interviews. Heather didn't want to get involved with the military trauma still hanging over her. Who knew what her discharge papers might reveal?

Get over it, soldier.

Those words, those wee little words, trickled across her consciousness as their story opened the eight o'clock morning news.

Chapter 9

The Request

"Are you still in the army?" the young reporter asked in her first interview of the day. They were back on the wharf in Advocate. Heather, Lester, Cliff, and Gert were gushing for the cameras, and Heather was prepared with answers she'd rehearsed most of the night.

"I'm on medical leave right now."

"You were in Afghanistan? Did you see action there?"

"Yes, we were in Kandahar, there was plenty of action on all sides."

"Is that where you learned first aid?"

"Yes."

Through all the interviews, she kept wanting to look over her shoulder to see if MPs were there instead of two television networks. The questions were mundane. The reporters weren't probing or looking for anything but a light story about heroes. They weren't digging into her service record or her two major military infractions, the memory of which brought back the roar of the major: "Suppose we let every girl act up like you. Bad behaviour is not tolerated."

The TV reporters were harried, the newspaper people more relaxed; television wanted footage. They posed Heather before the silvery tide in Advocate Harbour. The late morning sun made her hair glow. She wore no makeup, but her face was flushed with adrenalin. Part joy, because according to the last report, the young sailor was still alive. Part fear, because she just didn't know…

There was always a demand for heroes, one of the television reporters told her. More than a demand—a need, a necessity, to let us see the better side of ourselves. "Hero stories with the TV clips get wide coverage, and with a European connection," she was told by one reporter, "this a world story."

His words proved true immediately, as cards of congratulations arrived from Europe, Canada, and the US.

Heather realized she had no control over events.

The video on the wharf; there was so much of it, people knowing where she lived. Heather was facing a wired world. Technology had put her on a pedestal, with the story on news programs as well as online. Cards came addressed to only her name and Advocate Harbour, Nova Scotia. Norwegians wrote to her, some with broken English. A retired British army officer wrote to her, a waitress in Massachusetts praised her, a merchant in Quebec wanted to meet her. Letters and compliments came from people worried about the world who wanted to reach out to someone who had saved another human, who had done something worthy.

But the newly minted hero hid away. She waited at the Apple River Bar for the publicity deluge to subside. Lester went into Advocate Harbour every day or so to pick up the mail. It didn't take long before they learned the name of the young sailor: Erik Andres. His progress was reported in the press. In twenty days, he was out of Halifax hospital and back in Norway, recuperating. The media wanted a follow-up story; she refused. Yet the two of them, the ex-soldier and the young sailor, had shared such a traumatic experience, people wanted to put them together somehow. Heather didn't exactly understand, maybe it was their shared experience, but she was certain he would eventually write to her. So, she wasn't really surprised when his mother's letter arrived.

It was so deeply touching, the seven pages made Heather weep, but there was pride too. People could never say that she hadn't done anything worthwhile since leaving the military. If the army destroyed her reputation, at least she would have this. This life of a young foreigner she had held in her hands.

I know your language, his mother wrote, *but not precisely, so my neighbour will help me find the words, the English words. First there is the thank you.*

That is the most important thing for me to tell you. That love I feel for you, my wholehearted gratefulness. They are such feeble words to express what I have in my heart for you.

She reported her son, Erik, was healing from other wounds, including the broken rib and fractured ankle.

The idea grew in Heather. If she died tomorrow, at least she had performed one heroic act. It stuck with her over the next week. She had accomplished something good. Even if she was officially kicked out of the Canadian Army, she had done something meaningful on her own.

It was something, a life saved. She discounted similar acts performed in the desert; once she held down a Taliban chieftain while the medic worked on him. She knew he was a man who given half a chance would threaten to rape and murder her.

There were three of them pinning the big man while the medic worked on him. Heather held down his right arm and leg. The stink of his breath was on her face. The heat penetrated her helmet, wisps of sand brushing against the hot medic tent. She pretended it was waves. Oh, those hot, horrid days, the explosions, the people passive, the Afghan troops high on hashish. The entire war had been a shitshow. What miracle could save such a country? When bad memories rolled into her Heather would walk to the water and thank God that she had gotten out of there alive.

As the summer moved on towards autumn, there were still no military papers, no report on her condition, stating in black and white whether she was stable or nuts. Instead of military papers there came a sudden flurry of invitations, speaking engagements, invitations to charity luncheons not just in Advocate and Parrsboro but beyond the shore too. Even the ladies' bridge club of Truro wanted her to speak at their fundraiser for new card tables. She was asked to offer a few words to a newly formed girls' club in New Glasgow, on whatever subject she chose.

She continued to be a hero hiding, waiting month after month for her military release. That judgement that would decide her future. Every day she faced the same question: What would the army say? It was haunting her. What would the press report once they discovered their hero was unsuitable to be a soldier? Another flawed hero, joining the list.

She rejected every speaking invitation with a polite apology. She dreaded more arriving.

"Who do they think I am?" she asked Lester. "This is too much. I want to be, just to be…"

"Just to be what?" he inquired.

"More than anything, to be left alone so I can mend myself. That's all I need, a little time, to readjust myself to civilian life."

"I hope you make your home here in Advocate and of course here on the Bar, as long as this old shack can stand up to Mother Nature."

They were at the float house across the table from one another. Lester drew a deep breath and said, "There's a selfish reason I want you to stay, beside the fact I like having you around, and that I promised your mother." He got up and put a stick in the stove, although the fire didn't need it. "It's about Gus." He turned to her. "And me, and you. In case you don't know it, the house in Advocate is yours. I willed it to you."

Heather couldn't hide her astonishment. "I didn't know…I didn't know you even had a will."

Lester came back and sat down and looked at her over his glasses. "I'm sixty-one and I have a heart condition. I want things prepared, because the doc says…" He trailed off.

"What? What does the doctor say?"

"That I'm not going to live forever and to get my affairs in order."

Heather felt the alarm, the currents already electric. He was more than the titular head of her family; he was their linchpin. Who mended their scratches and scrapes, who taught and tended with care and patience? Lester was the closest man in her life. He was father and mother and uncle all in one. She could not lose him. Could not.

She tried to remain calm while a growing sense of unease was building within. Small tremors in her legs were already working. Thankfully, her legs were under the table. The tightening of the spine made her sit at attention.

Lester, trying his best to look casual, took his glasses off and was cleaning them.

"When did he tell you that, the doctor, when?"

"Don't be mad at me, now. It was a time ago."

"How long?"

"Three years ago." He sighed. "They said there was nothing they could do but keep a check on it. What good is that? I feel fine, but…"

"When was your last checkup?"

"Three years ago."

"You never went back?" Heather almost jumped to her feet. "Lester, tell me that's not true."

"What was the point?" he said, waving her away. "There was nothing they could do, but I had things to do." He paused again and drew a breath. "It's Gus. What happens to him when it's my turn to go to that great lobster supper in the sky?"

"Gert and Cliff, I suppose," Heather said, suddenly more unbalanced.

"They have no room with Marg there, and besides, they're long in the tooth and Gert isn't all that well herself."

Heather issued a rather mirthless laugh. "She might be better off to mind her own business, and stop being so pushy. You know, Mother always told me not to take anything off Gert. Not to let her push me around. But now I feel vulnerable in front of her. As an older sister, I think she lorded it over mother and caused a lot of mother's rather strident behaviour."

"Gert's got a heart of gold. Yes, she is loud and obnoxious at times, but my Dorothy loved her, and Cliff is a great guy." He shifted his weight in his chair, his big arms on the maple table across from her. He was almost as big as Cliff. His chair complained when he moved about.

"I don't think Gus would last long in a home. He's used to freedom, being outside. It's not that he can't function, but you know as well as anybody, his functioning is limited. You see my problem? I must try and protect that boy."

"You know," Heather responded, "that's a big order you're laying on me, if that's what you're doing. It's a lifetime commitment."

"No, I wouldn't do that. It is only a consideration. An option for you. You'd have a house and Gus adores you, but I'm practical. You may choose another career path in Halifax or someplace. I'm just saying, if you're staying here, you could make a life."

"The question is, doing what?" Heather countered. "I've a fine arts degree from California and a diploma from that school in Toronto. I've a dodgy medical discharge coming from the army that may claim I'm unemployable, emotionally maladjusted." There was quiet for a full three minutes. Heather felt the float house fill with tension.

"Here's the thing, Lester." Heather drew a deep breath, then hesitated a few more seconds to put her words in order. "If I can do it, if I can make a living here, I will try to do it. But no promises right now."

"That's all I can ask and more than I should." Lester was relieved the request was off his chest; it had weighed there like an anchor.

Heather was reeling from their conversation. She needed to ponder such an obligation, to think through things. She walked down to the dance floor. Thinking was always best in the fresh air, by the water. She sat and thought about her life while looking at Apple River Bay; a dark muddy gorge then, absent of water. The moon disappeared while trickling fingerlings ran down to the sea before it all began again. An owl was screeching across the empty bay, telling the world the water would be back in a few hours.

When the forces of nature are lessened, the water recedes into the wider Bay of Fundy. When the moon pulls, the tide answers, coming up the bay with more water than in all the rivers in the world. It is the great, twice-a-day miracle, billions of gallons moving north filling Chignecto Bay and streaming through the other finger of Fundy, the Minas Channel, with its treacherous rips that can make an anchor on a chain stand on top of the water. The tides keep pushing north past the old shipbuilding town of Parrsboro and up the coast to Five Islands, home of more famous sea captains. There was something about the movement of billions of gallons of water Heather always found magical, the shifting of water and earth. Her mother wasn't religious, but Heather still remembered her saying once, "It's a place, here at the Bar, that's close to God."

She sat on the dance floor and thought about her confusing, troubling future. She was cold, she supposed, but the feeling was ill defined, nothing like the desert. God, it could get cold in that wretched place. She was breathing on a regular basis now, as a military physician had instructed her after her first hearing, when she was hyperventilating over the unfairness of it all.

She was better off staying here. This was more home than anywhere else. She hardly remembered some of the places her mother had dragged her to when she was small; her memories from before she was seven were vague. Sometimes they seemed to live with a lot of people, other times by themselves. Gert told her once that Heather's mother had taken Heather as a small child to live in a commune in New Hampshire. Lester had driven down and gotten them. There was never a father in Heather's life, but there was always a family.

Heather pondered Lester's request. She could care for Gus. Many young women might not want to be tied down to an adult dependent because it would make them less available, but that was not a concern for Heather. She was fairly certain she would never marry. She wasn't a lesbian, and with very few exceptions, she really detested men. Those over her in the military were all men, and they had failed her and even failed in their responsibility towards her. Weren't they all in the same army, all on the same side? Why did she have to fight them? A sergeant got a kick in the testicles, and she was brought up on charges. He was groping her, hard groping, she called it. He was sent to the brig; she was sent to the shrink. Given medication. It didn't help, or maybe it made things worse, because her second offence was "striking a commissioned officer." She punched a second lieutenant so hard he landed on his back, knocking over a coat stand and making such a racket several people rushed into the room. Heather's hair was in disarray. The lieutenant had, without warning or permission, pushed her against a filing cabinet, kissed her while running his hands roughly along her body.

That was all before Afghanistan.

Chapter 10

Jealousy

Heather had so much to consider. What did she really want to do with her life? What was possible for her? The questions were suddenly pressing. It's not that they were new, but they were suddenly urgent, now that she knew about Lester's heart condition and the house in her name and Gus in her care. It was overwhelming, all of it.

But why shouldn't she stay here? Where would she find a more beautiful part of the world? This was home, maybe a safe harbour too.

If she could do anything, she would return to painting. It soothed her soul. Painting, the Bar, the float house, the dance floor all gave her peace. There was a tranquility to painting outdoors by woods and water; it was a fine hobby. But how many people could actually make a living doing it?

And anyway, peace wouldn't come until she could rid herself of her deeper demons. The trauma from Afghanistan, the military report. The army hazing, now the newly minted hero, all of it had to be take care of.

She didn't want to breathe and meditate her demons away. She had to face them head on.

Heather did some deep thinking. She knew in her heart, that vengeance against the Canadian Armed Forces was impossible. She had to rid herself of thoughts of revenge.

There was something more. Almost unidentifiably mystic. This coastal country with its mighty tides and low-slung mountains beaconed her on an emotional plane. No other place on earth ever had.

*

The seasons unfolded, with lobster and clams cooked in seaweed on the beach. An old bucket blackened by many cookouts bubbled up, extracting delicious aromas that could be caught only momentarily before being snatched away by intermittent sea breezes.

Heather healed under the sun in August and September and gained seven pounds.

"Actually, you look better," Lester told her when she complained she was getting fat. Gus, for better or worse, would always agree with Heather. "Yeah, you're getting fat," he said to her seriously.

"Nonsense," Lester declared. "She was too thin when she came home." He had told her many times she needed to put on weight.

"Is that why you're feeding me so well?"

In the first week of October, it was time to think about leaving the float house for another season and going home to Advocate for the winter. No one really wanted to go as long as the weather stayed pleasant. Sometimes September and October, with the hardwood colours afire, are the loveliest months of the year. Some years the bay is angry in the autumn and the Chignecto coast is swept by chill winds. No time for an outdoor bonfire.

One warm October evening with dark clouds rolling out of the east, Marg showed up with important news. She had been to a teacher orientation day for the new term, and she had discovered something Heather might like. Actually, she had two pieces of information. One, the school district had allocated funds for arts classes and a part-time art teacher in three schools in Cumberland County: Advocate Harbour, Parrsboro, and River Hebert.

"It's three days a week, but I think you might want to apply. It's right up your alley. I mean, you're qualified."

Heather couldn't even react before Marg moved on to her second piece of intelligence, obtained via the telephone, something they didn't have at the Bar, where even cell phones were spotty. And Heather had left hers in her military kit at a bus station. She did so intentionally, a route of escape from recent years.

"The Norwegian government wants to give you an award for the rescue. They left a number, it's from the premier's protocol person, here's her name."

Marg tried to hand her a piece of paper with a lady's name jotted down, but Heather rejected it, shaking her head. They were standing outside by Marg's car, behind the float house.

"Marg, please, I don't need that kind of publicity in my life right now."

"Maybe you don't, but they do," Marg said in her best schoolteacher tone. "It's good publicity for the province; nothing like a homemade hero. It's their job to find them and promote them."

There was something in Marg's voice besides the schoolteacher. An edge, a frosty crust. A crust covering what? It resembled bitterness or resentment. But Marg had no reason to envy Heather, and they both knew it. Just on the question of normal parents, Marg won hands down. She didn't have to lie on documents requiring the name of her father. "They need to find someone else, I can't. The publicity is already too much. Letters from Europe. I didn't ask for this."

They walked down past the dance floor, down the Bar past the empty trailers, used by the weekenders, past slender grass that grew on only one part of the Bar. They walked the half mile to the end of the Bar, where at the right time of day, the beach itself appears to be a great gravel wave about to roll into the sea. "What's wrong, Marg?"

Marg bit her lip, a custom since childhood.

"Listen, you may not want to do this, but you have to at least call them and explain why."

Heather took the paper with the name Marg had jotted down and put it in the pocket of her jeans. "I'll come up to Advocate in the morning and call. God, I'm sorry to be so disagreeable."

Marg stared straight at her. "I don't know, Heather, you seem pampered to me. Actually, you always were. I had parents and you didn't, yet…"

Marg looked away into nothing but darkness. Even the moon was hiding. No tide, no wind. They could hear each other breathing. "I was always a bit jealous of you," Marg said with quiet resignation. The bitterness had been carried away by the night.

"Not when we were kids. I don't believe that," Heather replied, feeling something coming up, catching in her throat.

"Yes, mostly then." Marg was walking away towards the float house, watching her steps in the night's blackness. "I don't feel jealous now. You're still prettier, and that's never been fair. You're slimmer and taller and blonder than me. For God's sake, Heather, you look like a Hollywood movie star in the national news, no wonder people are writing. I'm darker, shorter, and plumper, but I can't change that. I've accepted life. I've accepted who I am."

"Oh really, have you?" Heather said challengingly, with more bite than she intended, but she could not at the moment match Marg's new softer tone. "Accepted? I mean, really, Marg, you have accepted who you are?"

"Yes," Marg declared again, her tone just a little stiffened. "I'm a woman happy in her own skin. A woman who doesn't need marriage or a man in her life to be happy. My life experiences have left me with a very low libido, maybe. I was always jealous of you because I'm shallow and thin-skinned. I get that from Gert. I always hated the way Lester pampered you more than he did Boots and me. Boots knew it, but she joked about it. Nothing ever bothered her. Boots was big like Lester. I don't know, considering the size of my father, how I turned out so short, and you resemble…well, what's the point, the pretty girl gets the attention. I wonder if that's why you went into the military. Art school instead of teachers college, always something different."

"And you stayed," Heather shot back. "I went out and tried things, you didn't, so yes, you're settled and I'm not, I get it. But"—Heather drew a huge breath—"your *life experiences*? What life experiences, Marg? You had an affair with a married man."

"That was enough." Marg stumbled, hurrying to get to her car. "Maybe not enough for you, but plenty for me."

They walked back, Marg ahead by a few steps. She called over her shoulder, "Mom and Dad know about the award. I guess, based on your reaction, I shouldn't have told them, but they were sitting there when the call came. I just happened to be the one who picked up the phone."

Marg went to her car and left without another word. The float house was empty, Lester and Gus gone to Advocate. Heather sat at the kitchen table and permitted herself to feel the sensation of a dissolving lifelong friendship. They would remain friends or friendly, but some sisterly bonds were broken as the friendship wasn't equitable. One side felt something hostile.

Marg wasn't even out of the beach gravel the first time she swore and slapped the steering wheel. "Goddamn," she whispered. She hated herself sometimes. She didn't want to be her mother, yet her envious spirit, or spite, or whatever it was oozed out of her at times. She was a terrible bitch. She had always been jealous of Heather. She loved Heather like a sister, and envied her.

*

Within the hour, Cliff's big red truck, with enough chrome to blind a moose, came rumbling up behind the float house. Heather heard the crunching of the gravel. Three minutes behind them, Marg surprisingly arrived again.

Gert was beaming as she entered the kitchen.

"Oh Heather, we are so very proud of you, all this publicity, my goodness, all over the world, Clifford's boat, all over the world."

All that glowing from Gert reflected on Clifford, who looked as happy as a man does at the birth of his first child. Lester and Gus soon returned, and since the night was warm but very dark, Lester suggested a bonfire.

Any excuse would do. Within minutes they were all down on the dance floor, Gert and Cliff with their lawn chairs, the rest of them sitting on driftwood stumps. Gus had the radio on a Boston station and Lester and Heather were making a fire. Marg tried to take her mother aside, before she said anything to Heather, but Gert's self-control had evaporated.

"I'm so glad we got the Cape Islander painted and, now we're getting—you're getting—a medal, an award from Norway." Gert would not be stopped, brushing aside Marg's vain attempts to shush her. "How important that is for all of us," Gert gushed. "For the family."

Lester and Cliff watched like bystanders at a parade. Heather saw their faces fall when she told them, "I'm refusing it. Sorry, but I've had enough of the limelight." She changed the subject immediately, telling Gus to turn up the radio and find that Canadian station with the fiddle music. Lester had Gert up doing the polka; Marg and Heather didn't dance that night, although they had grown up dancing together, both light on their feet, but their dainty feet were not dancing. Even the rapid music from Ned Landry's fiddle could not lessen the disappointment that hung over them like sea mist. When the music stopped, the melancholy intensified. Gus always felt a change in the atmosphere, and he looked around, trying to decipher the emotional situation. Lester suddenly shuddered and Gert wrapped her long sweater tightly around her as a tidal breeze from the bay went through them. The moon came out and went again, playing hide-and-seek with emerging water. The tide was running, filling the bay and changing the environment, but it did nothing to push the wretchedness away. Something sad was floating in the misty atmosphere above and through this family.

But they didn't understand. They hadn't been there, hadn't been pushed against a filing cabinet. Hadn't put up with months of torment, teasing that became a wall that kept her outside her own platoon. She was part of the fighting, she was witness to the dying, but she missed out on the bonding of brothers, and, since 1989, sisters.

Could sisters ever bond in such a male enclave? She doubted it. She had been told, more than once, it was her fault. She was too pretty for the army. "That blond hair, hips and tits, what the hell did you expect?"

Her family just didn't know, and Heather couldn't find the words.

A sullenness came over Gert. "I'm not prying, but why, why would you not want it?"

Lester came to Heather's defense, so did Marg, and even Cliff told her to cool off, although he looked about ready to cry.

Lester piped up, "It's Heather's choice, and if she doesn't want to receive the award, she doesn't have to."

That was that, but Heather felt she needed to fill the void. She informed them she was going to start painting again. Gert sniffed and rather coldly declared, "That's nice."

Then they were going home, packing up at the end of a sour evening. Gert invited them for breakfast in the morning. Heather walked Marg to her car.

"Were you surprised to see me again tonight?" Marg asked.

"I rather surmised what happened," Heather said, relieved Marg was less tense and hostile. "You passed your parents on the road and knew they were headed here, and you turned around to…"

"Soften the blow," Marg said. "I knew Mom would have kittens when she heard. Dad too, but he wouldn't say so."

Cliff came by and hugged Heather briefly, but Heather could feel his disappointment.

Her family didn't know. Her heart ached. Lester looked at her with sympathy, but Gert had things to say. She hooked her arm around Heather's waist. "Take a walk with Auntie Gert."

It was another indication, an important milestone maybe in her emotional health. Heather felt she was healing. She could now almost laugh at this crazy, self-indulgent old lady who in Heather's early years had both tortured and nurtured her.

Clifford was ready to go home, but Gert left him sitting in the truck with the engine running. Auntie Gert was leading Heather down the few steps to the Bar. There was no pretext of collecting driftwood. This was straight talking, auntie to niece.

They stopped close to the dance floor and faced each other. In a split second, Gert put her hands together and looked skyward. Heather wanted to both laugh and cry. She wasn't sure if the skyward gaze was a call for heavenly intervention or strictly for show, another effect from a 1940s movie. Both were possible. Some of the cloud cover had disappeared, and the moon was spotty but permitted enough light to show how frail her aunt had become. It wasn't as noticeable indoors, where the lanterns improve everybody's appearance. Here on the Bar, secrets were difficult to conceal. Lester said it was the pull of the tides.

Gert stumbled on her words, but then came back blunt and forceful. "Heather, please reconsider. Please think about this. Don't throw the offer back in their faces as if you're an ungrateful child. This isn't just about you, Heather. It's about all of us. The entire family."

The word *family* sent a tremble through Heather, a feeling of comfort. Maybe Gert's voice reminded Heather of her mother when she said the word. They were all connected, weren't they? That link of blood and love.

Heather understood how much she was withholding from them. How incredibly important this was to her ageing aunt standing before her on the dark beach. But not just Gert. After all, wasn't she really the mouthpiece for Clifford and Lester? Two men she loved.

This was about more than Gert's shallow social prominence, more than ego. Heather suddenly felt the importance of this award to the people she loved. The family that had taken her in when her mother died. They could have passed her off to social services, but they were family.

It was that simple, and it struck her hard. How could she explain it? She wanted to avoid being more of a "hero" in case the army humiliated her, called her unfit for military service or emotionally imbalanced or whatever they might decide.

The look in Gert's eyes now was similar to a man she had run into, literally, almost knocking him down in the smoke and dust. He was a village man with blood on his forehead, and his village was destroyed. He'd waved at her. She thought he wanted help, but they were moving out, full speed. She abandoned his call for help.

Heather swallowed hard and thought about herself and what kind of person she wanted to be. *Strange, maybe*, she thought, *trying to find myself, to get some wholeness and maybe restore a little pride in my life.*

"Always be proud of who you are," her mother had told her more than once. "When they skin us, we're all the same."

Then Gert, trying to stay stern but close to tears, said, "Your mother would be so proud of you."

"I was just thinking of her," Heather said slowly, as if she didn't want the comfort of the thought to leave her. This was so difficult. She needed to get away, to be off by herself. She turned away from her aunt and started walking down the Bar, past twisted driftwood, its stubbing branches bleached bone white. The work of weather and tide, turning wood to pearl in the moonlight.

"Wait," Gert called, and Heather did what she was told. Gert caught up, breathing hard and angry. "You think family doesn't matter, maybe, but believe me"—she was spitting out her words with the rat-a-tat-tat of a military drummer—"believe me, it is the only thing that counts.

People who don't have families adopt families or adopt something in place of families."

"I don't think you're right about that." It was a declarative statement said quickly and firmly, and Heather wasn't through. "You know that Barbra Streisand song 'People'? About how lucky people are who need other people?"

Gert looked at her with a mystified expression and slowly, carefully, nodded.

"Well in my experience, Aunt Gert, you and Barbra are both wrong. The luckiest people are independent and don't need or rely on others. People who can stand on their own feet."

"Oh, and I suppose you're one of those?"

"No, not at all, but I wish I were sometimes. Family carries a certain burden, and frankly I'm burdened enough already. When you use the word *family*, it seems like family is now part of our daily repertoire. I never thought of us as a real family. Lester was Dad but not really, you were Mom but not really. It was all, for me, a little girl, not really a family. When Mom died, Lester was the kind father and you were the stern mother, sometimes unkind to me as a child."

Gert was furious now. She shook her head and sputtered, "Well, someone had to bring you up, didn't they? Someone had to teach you right from wrong, and I had to do it by remote control, from Spensers Island. Also, Miss Hero of the Moment, I raised Marg just the same way I tried with you. She turned out fine!"

Heather stepped back as if slapped. "And I'm not, is that it?"

"Marg is settled, you're not."

"Settled?" Heather shrieked. "Settled? Is that the same as satisfied?"

Gert had no answer, only a hard, teary-eyed glare witnessed when a cloud rolled away and the moon's silvery glow covered her face. She tried to turn, stumbled on the beach gravel, and Heather caught her and held her in a fast embrace.

Gert laid her head against Heather's cheek. She was softly crying. They held each other because they were family, by God; a strange, disjointed unit, but family nonetheless. Beyond them, Heather realized, who else cared about her?

"I'll accept the award, Gert," Heather whispered. Gert broke into loud sobs. They walked back to the float house, Gert sobbing all the way and leaning hard on Heather. Lester watched from the front door, his silhouette softened in the lamplight. Cliff got out of the truck and took his weeping wife, whose first wobbly words to him were, "She's g-g-going to accept it."

Cliff escorted his wife into the truck and whispered a soft thank you to Heather. They drove off to Spensers Island.

Chapter 11

Family Night

When Heather was settled back in Advocate Harbour she applied for the part-time teaching job. She listed her educational experience, her degree from California and her diploma from Toronto. She had taken out her oils and was painting again.

"Cliff is so happy with you," Lester said, "he'll build you a little studio if you like. Your own little building. There's enough room for a separate lot on the other side of the driveway, and you could hang a shingle in the summer, *Local art sold here*."

"That sounds very rustic and rather lovely," Heather said. "If I get this job, I'll take him up on that, but not for free. I'll pay."

Her first painting was of the story she'd heard many times over many years. With her easel out of mothballs and firmly planted in the sandy gravel, she wanted the tide as it was in the story, a good crisp wind blowing on shore, waist-high breakers rolling in. She would paint it as background, but the central aspect of the image had to be drawn from her imagination.

Heather was looking across Chignecto Bay at the New Brunswick coast. The colours were long past their prime, with only splotches of pale yellow that had been brilliant gold a few weeks ago. The last of the red maples, their leaves shredded to pieces, only stubborn strips clinging to branches.

The tractor gave her more trouble than the house itself, getting the waves just right, half the big wheels underwater. What was to become the float house was listing, a soggy wreck, with one end out of the water, the way Lester described it. The hind end was off in the painting too. She wanted it to be accurate, a depiction of that erstwhile struggle between man and nature.

*

They were well into autumn, and the wind had a nip to it. The waters in the bay were green and choppy. They knew without saying that this would be the last bonfire of the year. Cliff went to his truck and brought a bottle and Gert called him Clifford, as she did whenever he consumed alcohol. But Clifford was proposing a toast, something he had planned. He took out glasses from a wooden case and poured each of them a small dram.

"Here's to us!" he shouted, and they all replied, "Hear! Hear!" and downed the foul-tasting liquid. Clifford was then given his second warning, the usual after two drinks. It was Gert's traditional lecture: She would not be responsible for his truck if she had to drive, especially since she was having a glass of wine herself.

They had a great night. A family night, with the coming award glowing in their spirits. In most spirits, anyway. Gert was up demonstrating the Charleston. Lester showed them the rye waltz that the old Scots once embraced. Heather and Marg had their feet skipping to the polka, and Heather waltzed with Gus. They ate hot dogs and Gert's homemade doughnuts. They laughed and sang until the wind came off the water with the tide filling up Apple River Bay, making it look like a bay again and not a dry gully.

Finally, they could no longer ignore the chill. Gert and Cliff were folding the lightweight chairs to put back in Cliff's truck, the others were packing up the food, and Gus was putting down the aerial of his radio when Lester suddenly stopped them all in a voice meant to be heard; he was serious.

"I just want to tell you all…" Lester paused, waiting for them to quiet. He pressed his lips together and continued, "There is so much a man should say in his lifetime that he fails to say and regrets it later. This is my time to say something. I don't want to wait any longer. I don't want to lecture, and I'm not preaching." He attempted a smile. "It's just I want to thank you all for—well, for being you, I guess. When my Dorothy died, I was very down. I felt I didn't have much to live for. I searched around for what made life worth living, and it was you. All of you. Cliff, thanks for all for you've done for me. You're the best brother-in-law a guy could have."

Cliff, looking alarmed along with the others, nodded slightly. Lester paused for a second. "You too, Gert, for all the help with all the kids over the years. And Marg, thank you for your kindness, and Heather I love the fact you came back and made us a, oh, I don't know what you would call it, more cohesive family. My Dorothy is gone, and Boots is busy. But I still have all of you. I am happy about that; just wanted you all to know."

He turned without another word and walked up to the shanty. Gus followed his father, but unlike Lester, Gus kept looking back at them as he tried to determine what his father's words really meant. He saw the others as silhouettes in the lantern light, unmoving in startled silence. To all of them, it had sounded as if Lester was saying goodbye.

Chapter 12

Celebration

The awards ceremony was held at the Lieutenant Governor's official residence in downtown Halifax. The Honourable Bruce Stephen met the Hatfield family at the door.

Heather didn't know who wrote the speech that introduced her, but it was masterful in explaining the tension and excitement of running full speed with the spray high on all sides, shooting over the gunnels, the startled crew, the injured men, the wind and sea and blood.

When she rose to receive her award, she stood straight like a good soldier, but she was startled by the tremendous ovation from the 120 people present. She blinked and fought to stay strong.

She couldn't help feeling pride swell up with the ovation ringing in her ears. Her main worry was the military's conclusion on her mental and emotional wellbeing. She didn't want to end up looking like a fraud. How can an unfit soldier be a hero?

"Life experiences," she whispered to herself, a way to control her emotions as the Norwegian ambassador to Canada, a tall distinguished man with silver hair, placed his country's highest medal around Heather's neck. He said some nice words, lost in the emotion of the moment. She had only sobbed openly once. Gert sobbed continuously.

The reception afterward was less formal, and Heather was more relaxed knowing the ordeal was concluding. People mingled, wanting to meet her. Heather held her coffee in one hand and shook strangers' hands with the other while those around her carried on a host of conversations, brushed sandwich crumbs from themselves, and indulged in little cakes with the Canadian flag in white-and-red frosting. It was pleasant, and she felt strange and thankful the ceremony was almost over. Lieutenant Governor Bruce Stephen asked about her military experience, and she pretended not to hear his question. She asked him about his life own experiences, but when he persisted on the military, questioning her about her time in the armed forces, she wanted to finally shut him up. She did so by saying, "I was unsuitable to be a soldier."

He gave her a rather bemused appraisal, as if she might be pulling his leg.

While photographers were shooting Heather, a couple of military officers she didn't know stepped up to be in a picture with her. Their enthusiasm showed they were unaware of her military history. Suddenly, breaking through a circle of well-wishers, came a hand and a sharp tug on her sleeve. Gus was white with great alarm in his eyes.

"Dad needs you, he's sick." With that he bolted back to the door, with Heather and others following. A small group was gathering around someone on the ground outside. Elbowing past, she heard someone say, "Heart attack, or stroke."

No, no, no, please let it not be Lester. But she knew before she saw him.

He had already said his goodbyes.

Chapter 13

The Letter

Lester died the next morning in the Health Sciences Centre. Heather and Cliff were with him, and in his last hour of life, he hurriedly gave them instructions on the Cape Islander, on Gus, on the house, the garden, everything he could think of, all in a voice that didn't sound like Lester. Then he got very quiet and passed as if everything was done. Life completed.

It was a sombre, wretched time. Gus could not be constrained, and Marg lent a hand with him because Heather needed help with herself. The whole terrible time was made better by the kindness of neighbours in Advocate Harbour and people along the Parrsboro Shore. Lester knew a lot of folks as their friend and plumber, and it is custom in small places to look after one another with food and love and caring. It's taught in the churches along the shore, less than half filled now, some totally shuttered, but the values taught there in generations past survive in altered ways. The world Lester left behind was less religious but more humane. Call it the goodness of people. It showed itself in Advocate Harbour as food and help arrived at Heather's home by car and truck.

The funeral for Lester was large. The little church in Advocate Harbour was filled with mourners from along the shore and towns and villages in Cumberland County. Lester was a well-loved man. Gus did his best not to look like a crybaby. It was hard. Directly after they returned to Advocate, Gus had crawled off by himself several times to cry, not only for his father but for himself too. What would happen to him now? Heather had assured him she would always be with him, but still. She had gone away before and stayed a long time. How did Gus know she wouldn't go again? Boots had gone, Lester was gone; what would keep Heather here?

The church was full, and as the congregation sang Lester's favourite hymn, "The Old Rugged Cross," Gus looked quickly around. He was surprised to see Angus standing at the back. It comforted Gus knowing his only friend outside the family had come, particularly since he had never seen Angus in church before. But Angus had a private reason for attending Lester's service. It was important to him, being there in the crowded church, already sweltering.

Despite the unusual humidity it was a beautiful service. Gus didn't keep looking around anymore; he kept his head down so people wouldn't see he was crying as everyone sang the hymn. Heather was too, and so was Cliff in the hot October sun. Long ago in a place far away in his only year away from this coast, Lester had personally witnessed George Beverly Shea sing that famous hymn, and the church choirs along the shore had come together to offer a beautifully strong rendition for his funeral now. Gert, a slender tower in black, stood strong and stone faced, her thin lips disappearing in her rigidity. Cliff was weeping, his big moon face a fountain. Gus hung his head. Heather's arm was around his shoulders, hugging him tightly. Marg, chalk white, sat less rigidly than her mother. Gloria, her new friend, had shown up from Halifax.

Angus didn't stay for the reception, he slunk away. He was wearing his only suit coat. It had small grease stains in one or two places, but it wasn't bad for a man who had nothing. Something he had picked up along the way. What hadn't he fished out of the bay? Why were things always amiss? All he ever wanted had been denied him.

He wasn't stupid, and he really wasn't fooling himself. Gus might be the only fellow to hang around with him, but Angus really wasn't there to support his buddy. He knew what the driving force was, that deep desire from childhood, that longing to belong. Of course, there is a human longing to fit in, to have a place where you belong, but in Angus's case it was made stronger because even as a child he was alone. He had such a pull to be part of something loving, to be cared about, but it was always out of his reach. Such a strong desire denied empties out one's heart.

He searched the sky. There was a rain cloud way off, coming up from the Gulf of Maine and about to roll up the Bay of Fundy. He had a walk ahead of him. Some passing motorists might take pity and give him a lift. Most wouldn't, but people who had charity in their hearts, who understood the harshness of life, would stop and offer him a drive.

Angus was reeling as he walked along. He understood it was all fantasy, a daydream of sorts, and he knew why. What he didn't understand was the pull of it. The force in it being so strong. To attend a man's funeral, a man who didn't trust you. A man who he had never spoken more than a few dozen words to in his life, when they were on the water at night, when Lester accused him of stealing. Yet Lester had respect. People looked up to him. He was a man Angus wished to be himself, but never would reach such a stature.

Angus never teased Gus or poked fun at him. Gus had something Angus craved. Angus fantasized at times that he and Gus were brothers, and Lester was their father. Crazy, huh? Gus had a father and sisters. Angus longed for such a life. He may have been the only person in the world jealous of Gus Hatfield, but there you have it. To make it worse, much worse, Angus knew of Lester's feelings about him, because Gus had told him. It was during their conversation when Gus told Angus he had taken up for him. Taken his side. Angus didn't need to ask who was on the other side.

Angus had always wanted to prove himself to Lester, to show the man he wasn't useless, but how? Lester had caught him in the bay with lobster on his boat. They belonged to no one but the government of Canada, Angus told him, but Lester wasn't amused. What was the big deal? Sure, Angus poached a few lobster, but only to feed himself when he was hungry.

*

Heather's gloom was slightly lifted in late October when she learned she had the teaching position. It started at midterm in January, as a trial for one year. If the program was successful, extension was likely. Heather was both excited and nervous. She knew anticipation was worse than battle. In battle you may die, but in anticipation of it, you die a thousand deaths. About teaching, she needed to know a great deal, and she didn't have a clue about instructing children. She threw herself into the challenge. The days got better as Heather had her feet up by the kitchen stove reading every book she could get her hands on regarding instruction in the field of art and creativity for young children.

Still, the hollowness of the house was evident, and the nights were worse with the alarming lack of noise. When Lester got up from his chair, the chair issued a sigh. The floors creaked under his weight. Now the checkers never moved. She wished he would haunt the place, that she could hear his big frame moving about, sitting in his favourite chair watching the news. The checkerboard always nearby, awaiting Cliff to arrive.

Heather faced her new responsibilities as she had in the army, by pushing ahead, and that's what she was doing, from figuring out the best way to teach art to working up a schedule for Gus. He was going to be alone for several hours three days a week. She just wanted to make certain he ate properly. He had chores, too; firewood to bring in and the last of the potatoes to dig. It's not that Gus wasn't accustomed to being on his own, but Lester had always been nearby and keeping him busy.

Heather worried about Lester's Cape Islander, too.

Cliff advised her to sell. "Don't let it linger on the shore," he recommended.

She hesitated to tell Gus. Losing Lester was a terrible blow for him, and now the boat was disappearing from his life too. She tried to broach the subject a few times, but Gus wasn't taking the hint. She waited, not wanting to hurt him more than he was already hurting. Gus didn't need another loss. He considered the boat his own as much as Lester's. Maybe it was, but neither she nor Gus could look after the Cape Islander. Boats need upkeep, care, and attention. Yes, Lester let Gus go out in the bay by himself, and maybe others wouldn't have, but Lester always felt he had to let the boy live a life. He wouldn't deny his son the use of it. So of course Gus felt a certain ownership to the vessel. But he and Heather both had to face reality.

In November the letter she had been expecting arrived. The letter his mother said he would write when he was well enough. Heather knew it was from him even without looking at his name on the return address. She couldn't explain how, but she knew. It was timing, maybe; he'd had time to heal.

She had often thought about him, had seen his photograph in his hospital bed. She couldn't help wondering about his life in Norway. What kind of man he was. Certainly, the response from the Norwegians showed they cared for their countrymen. She'd received touching letters over the summer, from not only his mother but also a cousin and uncle too. However, Erik's message to her was so overwhelming she gasped when she read the second page. Gus watched with wide eyes. Gus could tell things about people.

Erik Andres's first page was what you might expect, two paragraphs of sincere and loving appreciation for saving him and a polite request she write to him. He had read that she was in the army. He had also read she was a single woman.

On the second page, Andres confessed that after seeing her on television he'd fallen in love with her. It was the strangest thing, he said; he'd been full of medications, painkillers and such, and after he finally saw her face, because his family had saved the broadcasts. He'd had dreams about her, strange, wonderful dreams. *I heard your voice on the boat and in my dreams.* He had read every article about the accident, every story about her, and he had saved them all. He picked up the best news photograph of her several times a day. He even imagined meeting her, he said. What words he would use.

I remember certain things from the boat. I couldn't see you, but your hands, I could feel them. I felt your fingers on my wound and I thanked you then, because I knew someone was helping me. But it was mainly the noise and spray and the motors and you above them all.

He remembered the spray on his face, the rough, bumpy ride, but mostly he remembered her hands on him. His dead friend, the first mate, was lying next to him on the deck. He could turn his head and see the white of his friend's face. His death made Erik realize, even in semi-consciousness, the peril they were all in. It both frightened him and increased his will to live.

He told her she was beautiful. He wanted to know all about her. Even if she was single, he assumed she had a partner, or boyfriend, because *no woman so striking is walking around by herself.*

Oh boy, Heather thought, *if he only knew.* With the exception of Angus and his lonely life, no one she knew, man nor woman, was walking so absolutely alone as she was.

Andres continued, *All the time in hospital, I read everything I could about the explosion and the beautiful woman who had save me. My main ambition in life is to meet you, Heather. I cannot wait for that day.* He was saving his money and looked forward to the day they could meet face to face.

He spoke English from childhood, but his writing was better in Norwegian, he told her. Heather found his English somehow endearing, but his declaration of love, his firm intention to come to Canada, scared her.

She was in some manner flattered, but more alarmed than anything else, and she had to put a stop to his intentions immediately. He was young, just twenty-four, and brash, but he seemed serious. His letter was so heartfelt, so genuine, due, she supposed, to their shared experience.

It was certainly not the first letter of affection she had received. Letters of endearment had come from much closer to home but were far less meaningful or sincere. A man in Port Greville had suggested they get together for coffee to see how things went. He had two dogs, and only as an afterthought he mentioned the same number of children.

I suppose you will turn me down. Others have. I say there is no hurt in trying, for reaching for the golden ring. I would care for you and wouldn't make you work too hard. Don't be scared of the ex-wife. She lives down the road but don't bother many. My offer holds until you turn me down.

She'd read that letter to Gert and Cliff. Their reactions couldn't have been more different, and the difference led to a disagreement. They often bickered like two old hens.

Heather closed her eyes and remembered her childhood, the first time she'd heard them going at it. She had been living with Lester about six months, adjusting to her first year in the Advocate School. Never mind pulling the blinds and asking for privacy; Gert and Cliff would bicker right in front of Heather. She was family. Of course, Gert did most of the bickering, chirping like a barn swallow. Cliff would stare at her, then softly say, in practiced, theatrical tone, "Darling, you're wrong."

"I'm not wrong!"

Cliff couldn't stop laughing as Heather read them the letter. Gert was wide-eyed, tittering, as if she was getting excited or sitting on a hotplate.

"Who is he?" Gert wanted to know, grabbing at the letter, but Cliff swiped it out of Heather's hand.

"You don't need to know. If you know, Spensers Island will know, and then the entire world is just waiting. Why do you even *want* to know? You planning to go see him?" Cliff couldn't stop laughing, and Gert got in a bigger snit when Heather wouldn't tell her the name. It wasn't the only such letter, and she regretted revealing it. Had she even read his name herself? Heather finished her coffee and left.

After that she didn't tell anyone about her other weird correspondence, such as the man from Maccan with three young children and ambitious plans. He admired her spirit, her courage. He had big ideas about local development of the tidal bore, that ankle-deep little wall of water that runs through the community ahead of the tide. He wanted to include Heather in his development as his spokesperson for his project. If she wanted children and matrimony, he was willing. A marriage proposal and a business partnership. All sight unseen. Scary.

There were letters of congratulations from many individuals, establishments, and institutions. A group photo, with *Congratulations* spelled in large print, from the customers and staff at Charlie's Bar and Grill in Chicago. There had been an article in a city magazine. One of the many telephone interviews she had done, over the summer. One of them was from Chicago. There were letters, all right, but no one talked about love or a shared experience.

No one except her young Norwegian. It bothered her that Erik was in her thoughts so much. But then, everything about the marine mishap and loss of life, that whole damn experience, was a nightmare that remained in the thoughts and dreams of those aboard the two Cape Islanders on that fateful day. Add that experience to desert warfare, which still haunted her memories.

Heather was frustrated and exasperated with Canada's military. She'd been waiting months to find out what the army would say about her. She could lose her teaching position overnight. But surely school officials would have checked her military record. Wouldn't they?

Heather could be classified as unfit for service. How did that fit with being a hero? Some zinger to carry through life. It dismayed Heather, but she had to smirk, too; no one had written her a love letter since grade three.

Erik's second letter arrived before she had finished writing back to his first. He told her he had given up the sea as too rough a life. He was more interested in owning a small garden centre and growing flowers. He had studied botany in university. He would soon save enough to meet her.

His plans were detailed. He was serious. He was coming.

The force of his message prompted a new urgency for Heather to respond. She wanted to be kind to him, and thoughtful, and to let him down gently. The first page of her letter read that way; now she hurried through the rest with a blunter tone.

You cannot come here. I have just lost my father and do not wish to see anyone. This is not the time. I am beginning a new teaching job. Another year would be better for everyone. Please understand.

His third letter was extremely sympathetic but no less determined. He had also lost his father. Then he too bordered on the blunt. *You have someone, is that it? Please tell me the truth. I am a grown man. I will love you always from afar.*

She wrote back that she had a cousin to care for and she did not plan to marry. *That*, she thought, *should cool his flames.*

It didn't. She was feeling his force as she had on the boat, his determination to live. She was beginning to understand he was not a man easily deterred. He had to come, he argued in his letter, just to see her, to lay his eyes on her, to hold her tightly. He had memories, bad dreams of the ship, the death of his captain and the first mate, his friend, his father's friend, the whiteness of him in death on the deck next to him. He was the man who'd gotten him on the ship in the first place.

Erik told her he wanted to go back to that island, to the waters around Isle Haute. His ship was damaged and tied up on the other shore.

It would be cut up for scrap. He understood all that, but it was cathartic somehow to return, to see where it had happened, at least.

But mostly to meet the woman who had put her hands on him.

The latest letter was more a plea than a love letter, and Heather was forced to reconsider her position. It seemed, upon reading and rereading his latest message, that Andres still needed her. She wouldn't want him to carry the dread around forever, like a heavy packsack. She knew it took a great deal of resolve and energy. She understood what dread was all about.

Heather was contemplating all this on a beautiful December day driving to the Bar with Gus, who had been solemn all morning. He had his moods, and Lester always said it was best just to leave him for a while and he'd come out of it.

Heather wasn't certain if this was the time to tell Gus that Cliff had found a buyer for Lester's boat. What words could she use, how could she frame it to be less hurtful? There was no easy way. She just had to say it.

They were late packing up the float house, taking the kitchen pots and pans that were going back to Advocate Harbour. Winter had already arrived. There was no time to waste, the buyer wanted to buy. Heather took a deep breath and began.

"Gussie, you know without Lester around we're going to have to do some things we don't like. You know that? Getting rid of Lester's boat is one of those things. People who fish all the time want to buy the boat. We need to sell it; you know that, don't you? We haven't the time or the money to keep up a fishing boat. You know that, right?"

Gus had the last of the pots in his hands, ready to place in a cardboard box. He looked at Heather with eyes full of alarm. He rose slowly, never taking his eyes off her. He put the pots on the counter. He was on the brink of tears.

"I know what's going to happen. I know." He flew out the door before he completely broke down.

Heather felt defeated. She slid down to the floor with her back against the wall, realizing she could have done a better job in breaking the news to him. It was one of those times she felt the world was closing in on her. Every day she expected her military papers. She had more jitters about teaching than she'd expected, and now how was she going to handle this? She had to do better with Gus, and she had to control her nervousness at the prospect of facing a classroom of six-year-olds. She stayed several minutes down on the kitchen floor. Dear God, how was she ever going to manage all this? Had Lester left her too much? She needed strength and clear thinking. Right now, Gus needed her, and the look in his eyes told Heather this was not one of those times you left him alone to settle.

She didn't have to go far to find him. Gus was sitting on the dance floor, his feet dangling over the side, not quite touching the beach gravel, his stoutness made more noticeable, his slumping frame showing how pudgy he was. Eating was one of Gus's few pleasures. As Heather approached, his squat body was sagging, and he had both arms bracing himself as if he might tip over and fall. His head seemed heavy, too heavy for his body. Gus was as silent as a person can be when wretchedly crying.

He didn't wait for her to reach him. "You think I don't know, but I know you're going to sell the boat and sell the house and move away."

His words came as a forceful gush, hitting Heather with a blast of unexpected accusations. It wasn't just the boat, it was everything. It was her.

Gus thought she was leaving because he and Angus had talked. "Dad said I would never be in a home. That's what he said. 'You'll never be in a home…as long as I can help it.'"

Gus was confused about that point. When Angus and Gus had discussed their futures, Angus talked about himself, not Gus, ending up with strangers. Gus had people. For Angus, the distinction between him and Gus was overwhelming. He never considered Gus could wind up alone. But Gus had spun off into his own thoughts by then.

Heather was speechless. All she could do was shake her head. "I'm not going anywhere," she finally gasped, embracing Gus, determined to handle this situation better. "Gussie, I'm not going anywhere." Her words were firm, solid, and she added in the same tone, "and if I was going anywhere, I would take you with me. You understand that, don't you? Lester left me the house and he left me you, and I'm grateful for both. I'm not leaving you. I never will." Heather released her embrace and bent down directly in front of him. "Besides, I have a teaching job. That's one of the changes I want to talk to you about."

"Where?" Gus asked.

"Here in Advocate, although I have to travel around. I'll be home at night, but you'll have to look after yourself some."

"But you're staying here with me?"

"Yes, I'm staying here with you."

"Forever?" Gus asked.

Heather looked over Apple River Bay. An emerging harvest moon was bringing in the tide, filling up little Apple River Bay and the river beyond. Heather sat down next to him, put her arm around his shoulders, and made her commitment to him.

"Yes, forever."

Chapter 14

The Visitor

With her commitment made, Gus became more relaxed, eventually telling Heather it was Angus who had told him about going to a home. She realized she had to confront Angus. He had to stop telling Gus tall tales that troubled him.

"Why?" Gus asked, looking alarmed when Heather asked where she could find Angus. She had seen him around all her life and knew he lived in the woods on the other side of Apple River Bay. But that was all. She wasn't going into the woods looking for him.

"I just want to talk to him," Heather replied, knowing he would want more.

"He didn't do nothing."

"He told you things that weren't true. I think he fills your head at times with nonsense."

"He doesn't," Gus replied and said nothing more.

It was another two weeks before Heather saw Angus walking along the road in Apple River. She stopped the car ahead of him and waited.

When he reached her, she got out and said, "Angus, can I have a word with you?"

Angus was also alarmed, similarly to his only friend. But he tried to hide both his alarm and his surprise. He shook his head in agreement and waited.

"It's about Gussie."

"You don't want me hanging about with him, is that it?"

"Well, Lester let Gus do his own thing and Gus obviously likes you. My concern is what you tell him."

Angus looked at Heather in a questioning manner.

"Telling him he was going to end up living with strangers, that was cruel."

Angus looked away from her for several seconds then back again, meeting her gaze. "I wasn't talking about Gus. Gus has family, why would I say that about him? It's me that's going to end up in such a place. Gus has family, he has people, I don't."

Heather had always heard Lester talking about Angus and his wasted life, but until that minute she had never realized what a completely lost soul he was. "Please don't say things that scare him" was all she could offer before getting back in her car.

"I never do," she heard Angus reply, and his words were so sincere she believed him.

*

Their lives settled into a routine in Advocate Harbour as winter began with blitzing wind off the water. After her pledge to Gus, he accepted their new reality. Cliff sold the Cape Islander. In her first weeks teaching Heather lost her initial nervousness in front of students. The little girls were sweet, and the little boys scanned her up and down with admiring eyes. The brave ones, and there were a few, wrote her juvenile notes of endearment. The little girls were more diligent, and many were interested in hearing about Heather's adventures. She told them a little, that she had been a soldier, and showed them on a map where she had been. Of course, the boys wanted to know if she had ever shot anyone. She wouldn't answer that question.

Heather loved teaching more than she expected. It made her wonder at times if she should have followed Marg into teachers college. Life would have been so much easier. She loved the children, there was joy to her job, and just doing something with her life was important. Maybe her mistakes had all begun when she refused to go into teaching.

Commuting over rural roads was a challenge in winter. She had almost struck a bear her first week on the job, driving back from Parrsboro in the dark, and the stupid animal was standing right in the middle of Allen Hill. Why wasn't it hibernating?

Heather arrived home later than usual on a stormy Thursday night. She had stayed longer than expected for a meeting. Route 209, locally called the Shulie Road, from River Hebert to Advocate Harbour, was snow clogged. It had been plowed hours earlier, but the snow was piling in, the flurries coming right at her windshield, making her eyes dance and her driving slow. She was glad to see Gus had remembered to turn on the outside lights. It was inky dark and the wind bit as she got out of the car.

She had no idea what was to come on that wintery January night or how her life was about to change. Gus came running out of the living room when he heard her, beckoning over his shoulder with a hitchhiker's thumb and a look on his face that said he had something that needed to be revealed immediately.

"He's here," Gus whispered, not waiting for Heather to take off her coat. "It's all right, he's all cleaned up. I made him come in and sit with me, so he didn't steal anything. We're going to watch *McHale's Navy*."

"Who is here?" she whispered back in the same conspiratorial tone, but didn't she know already? Hadn't he told her, repeatedly, he would be returning? His letters, his desires, his sheer force of personality…and there he was now in her peripheral vision, the dark form entering the kitchen. Here he was, and she was stupefied watching him approach. He was smiling, taller, more handsome than his pictures in the papers.

"Hallo, Heather," he said in a deep, rolling voice that carried something of the sea. His accented English contained a beautiful twang. His eyes were green.

"Hi, Erik." These two people, who didn't know each other but were emotionally connected. "Your eyes are green."

They stood motionless for a few seconds, staring at each other. She had saved his life and was suddenly a tongue-tied adolescent in front of him. He had done everything he said he would, and his kit, as he called it, was plunked on the kitchen floor. It looked like he planned to stay. He had come to her, out of need or something else.

"Your eyes are the colour of the sea." Her hands, slightly shaking, reached up and touched his face as if to make certain he was real. "Yes, like the water." She said it so softly she wasn't certain her words were audible. The thought vanished when he took her in his arms and kissed her. Not a peck on the cheek, but directly, squarely on her mouth. The kiss overwhelmed her, but she didn't pull away, because it was him. No man since art school had held her like this or kissed her with such intensity.

They released each other slowly, and only because Gus was tugging on her sleeve, complaining they were missing the show.

"He's right," Erik said breathlessly, releasing his embrace. "I did promise him I would watch television with him; it was the only way he would let me enter. He made certain I was clean, too, no blood. I had to take my coat off at the door and turn around for inspection."

In a state of disorientation Heather dished up dinner from the slow cooker and the three of them sat before the television, appearing almost like a normal family. Heather kept sneaking looks at Erik. She wanted to study him. There was so much of him. He was tall and broad-shouldered and so healthy looking. He was her masterpiece, she had saved him, and that single act pleased her, compensated for some of the misery of the past few years. She stopped peeking when she noticed he was doing the same to her.

They did the dishes while Gus watched television. When Gus went to bed, Heather and Erik sat at her kitchen table and talked until after midnight. They had exchanged letters, but those contained only a few of the million questions they had for each other. She briefly, at his urging, outlined her life in more detail. Lester, the most important man she had known, who had raised her since early childhood; Cliff, Gert, Marg, her mother. She told him the truth. Besides Lester, there was no father in her life and never had been. She mostly skipped the army, but he had read in the papers she had served in Afghanistan. She nodded but didn't go into details. He told her about Norway, its beauty, the mountains and fjords and rocky coasts. He had hiked through a lot of countries while in university but left in his third year for the adventure of going to sea.

Gus wasn't around to catch the magnetic intensity flying like electric spikes across the kitchen table. Erik was so sincere, so very heartfelt in his gratitude. Life radiated in those green eyes. Her hand was in his somehow; when did that happen? She didn't really know.

"I didn't know until now, it was your voice and not my imagination. You talked to me. You told me to stay alive, and I did." His smile was broad, his teeth even. He was a handsome young man.

Heather blinked several times and took a sip of her coffee. "You were bleeding badly," she answered. "I wanted you to live, and I was afraid you were not going to. I began speaking loudly over all the noise, ordering you to hang on; to live." She was clutching his hand suddenly, reliving the experience. They were both lost in the memory.

"That was the only word I heard coming from somewhere. That word *live*, as if it was an order, a command. I did not know where it came from. You were that voice carried by the wind, only I thought it was an angel."

"No angel," Heather replied. She was surprised to discover they were both teary eyed, more emotional than expected, in reliving their experience. Then they got giddy. They laughed. She was so very…what? Proud of him, proud he lived and smiled and talked. She didn't know him well but sensed that here was a man who loved life and was full of that love and the vitality to go with it.

Eventually, because it had to be asked, scary as it was, she probed his immediate intentions with a direct question.

"So, what are your plans?"

"If possible," he replied, looking at her with those green eyes, "I will stay here, then go to Halifax and look around, and then New Brunswick and look around. See the sights, you know."

"And after that, are you going back to Norway?"

He eyed her dejectedly. "Have you not understood my letters?" He told her he was staying here in Canada and had already applied for immigration. "I plan to begin a new life here, if possible."

"No, no, Erik, you cannot stay here with us. I would be happy to have you, but you cannot stay here."

He was pleading his case as if she were the immigration board. "I want to establish small garden centre. I have two years of university botany. I have a little business background, not much but a little, and maybe I will purchase small piece of land." He stopped and added, "Near you."

"No," she heard herself say, shaking her head vigorously and hating every word she was saying. "I'm a single woman, just starting a teaching job. I can't have a strange man, I don't mean strange, I mean, I mean…"

He stopped her. "I will not cause you problems, Heather, but at least let me know you a bit. I owe you everything."

She got up from the table and smiled at him. "I think you've given me something too. I'm proud of myself just seeing you alive."

She made up the bed for him on the living room sofa. She just couldn't let him have Lester's room. It was empty, but it was Lester's. Heather hadn't taken it for herself or turned it over to Gus. The biggest bedroom in the house stood empty yet, the inhospitable innkeeper was turning away her special guest, yet permitting the guest to kiss her repeatedly. They were long, lingering kisses, too; more desiring than she expected.

Her head was spinning as she walked up the stairs and got into bed full of conflict and regret. What she regretted was already evident, the withholding of Lester's bedroom. Why? Was there something deeper, such as Heather not really trusting herself? Was it that she didn't trust herself or her own feelings? She felt rotten for treating him so incredibly inhospitably, making him sleep on a sofa. This man was not a stranger. They had shared a unique experience. Did that explain things? She writhed that night, tossing and turning and whispering new commitments to herself.

She finally unearthed the truth around twenty after three. A single woman with a teaching job? The impropriety of a man staying with her was nonsense. Who the hell would care about that? Unmarried people lived together all over the country. It was a ruse, an excuse. The real reason had finally come to the surface.

She was scared. Frightened of herself and her surprising sudden attraction to him, alarmed how attached she was to this young Norwegian. She was almost five years older than him. Restless in her bedcovers, she had a disturbing dream, her as an old lady alone, then running in the sands of Afghanistan, carrying a young man in her arms. His blood was running through her fingers. When she looked down on the man it was Erik. She awoke crying and didn't know why. The army shrinks had suggested she had mild PTSD due to combat, but she knew she had been recovering slowly. The tremors had not completely ceased, particularly in the last month. Teaching had been a good diversion.

Heather felt she was getting her life back but wasn't ready to trust herself with these feelings. What did she feel or see in this attraction that she didn't trust? Lester would tell her to trust her instincts. But those instincts may lead her astray.

She went to the bathroom at twenty to four and washed her face. It felt good to have a man in the house. It gave her comfort that she'd never needed or sought such company, but there it was. Heather needed to know, to discover if this was more than a passing attraction, because it felt like more, much more. In the morning, she would tell him to stay. She would turn over Lester's room to him. Erik had come all this way, across the ocean, hitchhiked down the Parrsboro Shore. People had been obliging, he had said. He also told her he had his kit and was comfortable out of doors.

In their long hours of talking the night before, she asked him if he was afraid of freezing to death outdoors in the winter. He laughed in that warm, soft, rolling voice of his, telling her he had travelled over much of Europe in the winter.

She rose early, numb and sleepless, earlier than usual, before the alarm clock told her to rise. Heather felt she was the bitch from hell for refusing him a proper bed when there was an empty bedroom. This feeling of fright conflicted with that lingering kiss goodnight before she climbed the stairs. It was so confusing in many respects. Yet she had withheld many things she wished to tell him. It wasn't his business, her experience in the army, in Afghanistan, but she wanted to tell him, wanted him to understand her completely. Why, when she feared her own feelings? She could not explain things rolling around in her unsettled mind. She wanted to bare her breast to him, to show him her military record, when it ever arrived. She desired to be a better person, an open, honest person. Heather felt for some reason she needed to tell him of her two infractions, one withdrawn, one not. Heather had tried to hide away when she first came home. She didn't phone any of her old girlfriends; most were gone, anyway, working in careers or jobs, or had married and moved away. But she had stayed away from the few who stuck around, hiding out at the float house. Then the shipwreck happened, and there was no more hiding. Too many people wanted her, and their wants were different. Erik wanted her for her, not to speak or be displayed. She felt Erik's wants were different. He wanted her.

Heather was by nature a gracious person. She would not be rude or aggressive, and she relented to pleas for interviews. She was forced to have one foot in the public realm, at least for telephone interviews, and to heal herself at the same time by dealing with the tremors. She was determined to show a better side of herself. "Fear of your own emotions is no excuse for bad manners," she told herself.

That silly piece of nonsense sounded like her mother, but then her mum could demonstrate extremely poor manners when she wanted to, so it wasn't her. She rose sleepy but with a new conviction. To make up for what she considered extreme discourtesy. Yes, of course she was confused. She had been kissing him, which certainly wasn't inhospitable. The other side of the coin was different. She didn't want to be involved with him. It was too overwhelming. But still, Heather Hatfield, newly minted hero, veteran of foreign wars, took extra care with her makeup and chose what dress to wear, one she'd never worn to class before. The green one, the same as his eyes.

Heather was suddenly nervous about something as she looked in the mirror. She sat on the side of the bed for a moment, trying to understand the cause of the jitters. Of course, it was him. What else? She shook her head. One final look in the mirror and she went downstairs, her shoes in her hand. It was barely light out. Heather would rouse him with a nice breakfast before heading off to teach in Parrsboro, and then they would spend the weekend together. They would get to know each other better. Maybe then this silly attraction would end, or she would find him wanting in some manner.

As she went through the living room to the kitchen, Heather took a quick glance at the sofa to see if Erik might be awake, and…he was gone.

The bedcovers were neatly folded and piled together, but he, his boots, his kit, everything, had left her. Something ratcheted in her heart as if the vital organ had been struck by a blunt object. Heather braced herself again the wall. She felt an inexplicable loss over something she had never possessed. How could that wound the heart? Heather ran to the kitchen, a flicker of hope he was sitting in the dark. But of course he wasn't. Who sits in the dark?

She grabbed her coat and the flashlight and was out the door in a shot. She had tracked the Taliban in Afghanistan, followed the warlords through rock and sand. The snowy driveway was easier. He hadn't left all that long ago. The tracks turned left; he was going back towards Parrsboro, retracing his steps. Heather rushed everything, including Gus. She roused him for breakfast. No time for the slow cooker, not this morning. If she hurried, she might yet catch him on the road, as there was little traffic. Why did it matter so much? Yet it did. He was her handiwork, she had made him new, and suddenly she wanted him near, not driven away by the shrew she had become.

She sped along, hoping to see him in Advocate Harbour, but there was no sign of a hitchhiker in this weather at this hour. Every third house had its lights on, even the dark and shuttered houses had smoke rising from the chimneys. This was wood-burning country. A man was using a tractor to clear his driveway. The wind sweeping down from the Advocate cemetery blew most of the snow at Lester's house, so her driveway had been mostly clear. The snow was high on both sides of the road where the plows had pushed it. A hitchhiker would have to be standing almost in the middle of the road to be seen. He was nowhere, and as she reached the end of the village, she drove with her hands tightened on the steering wheel. Heather even cast a glance behind the houses at the old Acadian dikes and the slate gray waters of Cobequid Bay behind them.

So scared only hours ago, even of herself, she was the fearless fighter now. The sleepless night was not for nothing. Her tiredness had turned into a driving force. She was coming up to the turnoff to Spensers Island when she saw a dark figure on the road. Was it him? Yes. Yes, it was him; it was.

Erik was prepared to jump aside when Heather burrowed into the snowbank and came to a frantic stop less than a foot from him. She threw open the door and jumped out. In a split second everything transformed. She was suddenly livid.

"Why did you leave like that?" She was spitting out her words. "Leaving without even a note or anything, where did you think you were going? I thought you came all this way to see me, and to leave like that after all, you know, the…"

The kissing had rekindled the knowledge that she was more than a hollow core. The kissing had unearthed the feelings and sensations she had buried in the sands of Afghanistan.

Despite the crisp morning air, her face was hot, and she would have continued with her tirade if not for the look of extreme concern in his eyes.

"Heather, I left a note for you on top of the bedding."

The heat now was embarrassment. She hadn't looked closely at the bedding, hadn't seen a note. She closed her eyes as he took her in his arms. "Where are you going?" Her voice had the moan of a lost child because she felt childlike with his arms around her as a parent consoles a hurting youngster. He kissed her then and reminded her of his plans while they embraced with her car still running and the driver's door open. He was going to Halifax to look around, and then to New Brunswick to have a look around there.

"So you're coming back? You're not going for good?"

"Yes, I will come back, and I will find a place to live."

"No, no, you can stay with us. I was wrong. You can have Lester's room."

"But your reputation?" He said he understood her position, but she didn't want to hear any more and kissed him again.

That was when Minky Morrison drove by in his big lumber truck. The lumber companies were destroying another forest and he had trucking to do. But by God, it's not every day you see a car on the road, its engine running, the driver's door wide open, and two people kissing outside like they badly needed a hotel room.

The second motorist to spy the kissing couple, right after Minky, was Marg, also on her way to school in Parrsboro. Marg jerked her head around so quickly she wrenched her neck, which made her sour mood even more unpleasant. She gave her steering wheel a hard slap.

"There she is, our beauty queen, the girl who wants to be just left alone, making a public spectacle of herself." The second slap hurt her hand. Marg, with hurting hands and paining neck, was also ashamed of herself. She understood that at the very core of her frustration was a spot of pure jealousy. Heather had always been so carefree in her youth, willing to go places and do things. Now she was a hero. *And there's me,* Marg thought. *I stayed and did what was expected, so why am I so unhappy with my life?* She rubbed her neck. It would be a long day.

There is an unofficial courier service along the Parrsboro Shore. Word of mouth can travel fast, especially when it's the latest quirky bit of gossip. Minky told Betty at the store on his second trip through Advocate that day. Betty told Codfish Thompson, who passed the news along to Mrs. Generous Smith, who informed Marion Fletcher, who told her brother Alton, who informed Cliff, who told his wife and immediately wished he hadn't. Cliff put his foot down Friday night and told Gert to leave Heather alone.

"But who was she kissing?"

"It doesn't matter the who of it, leave her alone." Cliff didn't put his foot down very often, as it was usually a fruitless effort. But with Lester gone he felt it was his duty to protect Heather. Things had been rocky between Gert and Marg. First it was over Marg's lack of serious romance and non-production of babies. Now it was all about Gloria, and Gert wanted to know why her only daughter was spending so much time, every weekend now, in Halifax.

Gert bowed her head Friday night and dutifully listened as if she was about to obey every word said by her husband. That obedience lasted twelve hours. The next morning, when Cliff's red truck left the yard, Gert slipped a pan of brownies into the oven and went to get dressed. She had visiting to do.

Chapter 15

Marg's Announcement

It was a fine Saturday morning; the snow had stopped during the night and Heather considered painting outdoors for an hour or so in the sun. Her plan was to spend a good part of the day with her brushes in hand. However, before ten thirty, she heard a car in the yard. Hardly surprising it was Gert. Of course, Gert had heard the news.

Marg had mentioned it at school rather unkindly. "I saw you smooching on the side of the road this morning, Miss I Want to Be Left Alone." Marg was gone before Heather could respond, but a new buoyancy protected Heather from anger or disappointment. Marg was having a hard time with life.

It had passed through Heather's mind more than once that Marg was fighting something within, that there was some internal struggle going on. She remembered during their last walk on the beach, Marg saying, "I love my Dad, don't want to hurt him, but Mother suspects things. She knows the truth. Dad is looking at her and there is tension between them. Dad is wondering what's going on. Awful thoughts have gone through my mind in recent months. I don't want to hurt anybody, but I've got to make a decision about my future, how I am going to live and who I truly am."

So, Gert's arrival now, on Saturday morning, was really no surprise. The painting would wait as Heather opened the door for her aunt and Gus retrieved the brownies.

Most Maritimers prefer the kitchen for social occasions, so Gert plunked herself down at the table while Heather made coffee. Gus was watching cartoons in the living room. Heather reminded him the wood box was empty.

Gert was anxious. Why did she have to wait to learn things? She'd been dying to call Friday night, but she couldn't with Clifford sitting around, watching her like a hawk. There was news here, and Gert wanted to know the details. Emotions, secret urges, dreams, ambitions, or private hurts. Gert was extremely interested in what had happened that brought a man into Heather's life so quickly. Who was he? Where did he come from? Could he be that sailor from Norway?

Heather was going through some transition. Gert could see that immediately in the manner her niece carried herself; something was unwound, relaxed. It was all good, Gert thought. *Maybe it's not too late, maybe she'll marry yet, have children. My grandchildren, almost.* She rolled around the term *grandnieces*.

Below her surface lay Gert's deeper layer of turmoil, that hidden room where things are kept, things we never want revealed. Hateful or lustful thoughts, ambitions, desires we're ashamed of. The deeper layer in Gert was the twitching, troubling concern close to her heart.

"So, Heather, what's new with you?"

Gert waited until Heather was seated at the kitchen table. The first question came while she was at the counter with her back to Gert, allowing Heather to smile to herself.

"Oh, nothing much, Aunt Gert. What's new with you?"

Gert twisted in her chair. She was jittery, like a witness in court testifying against her in-laws, crossing and uncrossing her legs under the table. She'd never considered herself a gossip. But she had a driving desire to impress others, mostly her peers, the bridge types, with her inside information on any matter. Gert considered herself the major fount of community information concerning the Parrsboro Shore.

"Heather, please, don't play games with me. I know there is someone in your life. Is it someone you met in the army?"

"Army? Hardly, Aunt Gert. Why would you think that?" She was teasing her aunt and it was one of the few times she had done so. More importantly, she had used the word *army* in a lighthearted manner. Heather was on a plateau that had been out of reach in recent years. She knew what it was—joy. Pure, unadulterated joy.

"Heather, you were kissing someone, half the village knows. Don't you have an obligation to disclose such things to your family?"

"No, not really, I don't." She sat down across the table, sipped her coffee, and waited. Gert next played the age card, which she hated using, but she wanted to hurry things along.

"Heather, I'm an old lady, have sympathy for me. I just want to make sure he is right for you, it's part of—"

Was she going to say "a mother's duty"? She stopped short of that.

"You don't need to vet him, Aunt Gert, he's passed muster already. I vetted him and found him satisfactory."

Gert took a deep breath, there was so much she wanted to know, wanted to say. She raised her head as her chest swelled and she peered into Heather's eyes. "Is he your sailor? He's come?"

"Yes, he was here."

The past tense drove Gert crazy. "'Was'? He's gone? Where? He's coming back, isn't he? We want to meet him, where did he go?"

Heather put down her coffee. "He's in Halifax, and then he's going to New Brunswick."

"But—but—why? When is he coming back? He's part of the story, our story."

"He's coming back in ten days."

"Really?" Gert pushed her chair closer. "He said that? You believe him?"

"Let me put it this way, Aunt Gert. I witnessed him fight for his life. I've corresponded with him. We sat at this table and talked into the night. He is a determined man who does what he says. He'll be back."

"Oh, Heather, you were kissing him, there may be babies yet, it's not too late." Gert was clasping her hands together as if she were going to break into a hymn.

Heather laughed. "Don't get ahead of yourself, Aunt Gert."

But Gert wasn't laughing with her, or even showing any signs of happiness. The environment at the table was swiftly changing. Gert's curiosity had been sated for now, so only the deeper pain remained. She was hopeful there might be babies. Having her pressing question answered, there was only the rest of her worries to bubble to the surface. She sighed. "If only Marg would find somebody."

Heather smiled, knowing full well what Gert was thinking: *"Then I wouldn't have to settle for secondhand grandkids."*

"If only Marg would cooperate," Gert said. "I was almost ready to acccpt an illegitimate child if she had one. What's wrong with you women?"

Gert's moods could change faster than a nor'easter. Heather knew the signs: Gert was building up a head of steam, going into one of her furies, which would be followed by a string of weepy apologies.

"Almost thirty and neither of you have produced a thing. Not a goddamn thing." It was a ruse, the grandchild excuse she was waving around on her high-and-mighty emotional flagpole. Oh, she desperately wanted grandkids, all right. She and Marg had had many talks about them, many arguments, but that was a cover. Sitting in Heather's kitchen, Gert wanted to know, or did know, or thought she knew, something about her daughter—but she wanted confirmation.

The distress flowed out of Gert as the spring tides flowed out of the Bay of Fundy, splattering sobs on her cheeks, her voice the low, weeping moan of an approaching sea. But the tide stopped as quickly as it began. Gert straightened up, pulled herself together, and finally, with a ramrod back and in a half octave above a sob, declared, "My daughter is gay."

Heather bit her lip. Would Gert have a breakdown in her kitchen? "Marg has to live her own life, Aunt Gert. I suspect that affair with a married man changed Marg, hurt her deeply. Maybe she's found her new self."

After five minutes for more coffee and another wet tide and one more time recovering her composure, Gert soldiered on.

"It's not that I don't want my daughter to have a happy life. But damn it, why me, why us, who can afford to spoil grandchildren?"

"Look, Gert." Heather's tone was firm. "You should know by now you can't own children, and spoiling isn't a good idea. I think you should let Marg live her own life. There are other things you can do for children if you want to. There are starving children all over the world. I've seen that for myself."

Gert sighed and stayed silent a moment. Heather thought she was defeated but realized how silly she was when the phoenix rose from the ashes.

In other words, Gert made a comeback. Raising her chin and her spine straight as if making herself taller, she sputtered, "I don't like that Gloria. She took my daughter and—"

Heather put up her hand. "No, Aunt Gert, she did not. Marg wouldn't be there if she didn't want to be, you should know better."

"I don't like her anyway," Gert huffed. "She's a snob."

Heather forced herself not to laugh at Gert calling someone a snob. "It would be better for Marg if you got along with her partner," Heather replied, feeling out of her depth with such a delicate conversation.

Gert continued. "She's been spending all her time with Gloria instead of looking for a man."

"Good men are hard to find," Heather replied.

"How come other women can find them if they're so damn hard to find?"

"Maybe they're less picky or just luckier in life."

"Or some people are more eccentric."

"What does that mean?" Heather asked, getting weary of Gert's intensity.

"Well," Gert drew in her chest, "kissing someone with your car eating up expensive gasoline is rather—I don't know, Heather, rather unusual, isn't it?"

*

Surprisingly, Marg called the next morning. She had some news and invited Heather for coffee. "It's a nice day if you want another beach walk."

There was the first hint of spring in the air, meaning spring tides would soon bring more water and higher tides. They had often seen the damage from past years, with pockmarks and new gouges out of the soft cliffs of the Chignecto coast. There was a warm breeze as Heather arrived at Marg's, it was a perfect day.

They smiled at each other at the front door and Marg asked, "Do you want a hat in case the wind comes up?"

Heather pulled a woollen toque out of her pocket and off they went, these childhood friends, walking the beach today and suspecting they were at the cusp of something new. Heather thought perhaps they were both heading into new and separate adventures.

You can see for miles on a winter beach along this coastal area of Eastern Canada, where the waters of the Bay of Fundy branch off into Chignecto Bay and Minas Basin. You can walk for hours and never spy another human. They were alone on a windswept beach, but an astute observer with knowledge of these two women might notice their strides were different. There was less hesitation in movement, a freer swinging of arms, an easier motion.

"I'm sorry, Heather, for the way I spoke to you at school on Friday. I'm too much like my mother. I badly need a change, so I have an announcement to make." Marg gave a little laugh. "It was always you making announcements. Remember, you were always going off somewhere, to art school in Toronto—Lester threw a big party for you—then another art school in California. Another party for our girl going away. Then you were back and going into the army. Another announcement, another party to honour Heather."

"Those parties weren't any more for me than for you, Marg. They were for all of us."

"True, technically that's true, but you were the star of the show."

They walked on in silence. The tide was all the way out, far down the beach, and so were the seabirds. Patches of rotted snow appeared as clusters of white clover, in some cases almost indistinguishable from the white backs of the herring gulls. They were suddenly both looking hard at the water that wasn't there, wishing, on Heather's part at least, that it was next to her, lapping at her feet. They walked several steps in silence as if Marg was organizing things in her mind. She finally continued. "So, today it's my announcement, and I don't expect a party. I've resigned my teaching position in Parrsboro. I'm taking a job in the west end of Halifax. It's a good school."

"Marg, congratulations." Heather hugged her. "I'll miss you.

"Why? I'm a bitch, an unhappy woman sinking into her middle years, that's the way my mother puts it."

"Marg, your life isn't over. I'm so happy for you."

"Thank you, Heather."

They embraced as they did as excited teenagers years ago. Then, arm in arm, friends and sisters again strode up the empty beach.

"Gert visited yesterday," Heather said and Marg snickered.

"Yes, she can't understand. Coming out, if that's what I'm doing, well let's just say it wasn't a pleasant scene last night, everything came to a head. Dad sitting in the corner about ready to cry, and Mom. Well, you know Gert. There are things I said to her and other things I wanted to say but didn't. Honestly, I'm not certain who I am or what I am. But if someone makes you happy, someone you are comfortable with, who you love even if you're not supposed to…I must live my own life."

"You'll be fine," Heather said. They embraced again, and Heather felt they had that morning healed their relationship, or at least they had put each other on a new level of understanding.

"I don't know if Mom will ever come around if Gloria and I…well, I just don't know." Marg looked a long way down the beach, ready to cry.

"Let's keep walking and meet the tide," Heather replied. "It's always peaceful near the water."

Chapter 16

Leaving the Nest

They walked down the beach to meet the incoming tide.

"It's Gussie's birthday next weekend. I want to do something special for him. He loves lobster, so I'll fix a nice dinner for us. I'd like you all to come."

Marg smiled. "He gets very excited on his birthday. Remember his fifteenth?"

"Yes," Heather replied, "and it's rather special this year, he's thirty-five. Can you imagine? Outside of the weight he's put on, he doesn't appear much different than he ever did."

"Not as many wrinkles as some of us," Marg said, lightly tapping her face to make a point, "and speaking of weight, have a looked at my hips? Well, even if you haven't noticed, Gert has. Oh yes, she points it out. She's terrified I'm becoming so unattractive no man will want me, so I have to settle for a woman. Can you imagine?" Marg issued a mirthless laugh. "I want someone in my life I trust. Can you understand that? Stability is more important than…" Marg paused, searching for words.

"Eternal pledges of love?" Heather supplied.

Marg nodded and would have said more but the tide was up to them and forced a short march back up the beach. "I put a big priority on comfort," Marg said once they were walking by the waves. "I don't want to spend my life worrying if he's going to leave me. I did it once, never again. I wasted enough years, enough of that, enough of living with my mother, too. Yet I worry in a way that this jump I'm making both in my teaching and personal life is just an escape from Gert. Running away from my own mother."

"I don't think you'd be the first daughter to do that," Heather replied.

Marg hesitated, then said, "I love Gloria. It's taken me a long time to say that out loud or even to myself, but it's true. She gives me what I haven't had these past years, and I want what she does for me without trying. She makes me happy." Marg looked at Heather and continued, "I ask you, is there anything more important, more basic to human need than the warmth and security of a satisfying contentment if you want it? Without it, there's something missing. I know which children come from happy homes and which don't. You can't fool a schoolteacher. There are little signs, and you become, after a few years, able to read them. The children who are neglected are easy to pick out because of their clothes or general appearance, but the ones who hide their unhappiness because of some neglect or harshness at home take more observation."

"I enjoy teaching more than I imagined," Heather said. "Maybe I should have followed you after all."

Marg guffawed. "Too late now." This time they laughed about it. For years it had been a touchy subject for Marg, and now she was smiling. That was a good sign from a woman who had smiled and laughed less in recent years. Heather consider it part of the water, tides, sea air, and healing. In her mind they were always part of making things better.

They stood on the coast looking into the bay. The aroma of the incoming tide was salty foam and seaweed and a hint of pine and wet wood, as if the wind was coming off the forest, not the water. That slight trace of evergreen might be from a forest across the bay or far, far away.

"I love the sea air," Marg said, and Heather knew exactly what she met. The healing balm of the coast. "This magical place," as Lester put it.

A dory came into view, its outboard motor making only a muffled hum in the distance. They stood facing the water and let the weariness of the past melt away in the breeze.

They parted with a hug and a promise by Marg to bring her parents to Gus's birthday party the next Saturday afternoon. Driving back to Advocate Harbour, Heather was relieved. Marg was making a move. Only time would tell if it was the right move. It had taken Marg most of her twenties to make it, but the decision had been made. She was finally leaving the nest.

Chapter 17

Gus's Birthday

Heather debated about Gus's party. Should it be a surprise? Should she invite Angus? She decided she was not going to make it a surprise. Gus wasn't stupid. He knew his birthday was coming, and he would be expecting a gift or something. Better to tell him so he could look forward to a celebration.

Gus's eyes grew wider when she told him. He hadn't had a real birthday party in years, but Heather said thirty-five was special. Gus didn't know about anything special, but he was more than ready for a party with lobster. It had been a while since they'd had a real party, an indoor party, with all the decorations. Gus's sister Boots had been at his last birthday bash. She wouldn't be there for this one but always sent him a gift, even when she was a poor university student.

It was satisfying for Heather to see Gus so happy. Happiness can be contagious, can spread itself around like coastal fog. Gus beamed when the world was good to him.

"Gert and Cliff are coming, and Marg will bring her fiddle. I've already invited them."

Then Gus gave Heather a total change of expression, his face turning serious, and he said something unexpected. "Can I invite Angus? He's never been to a birthday party."

Gus waited for her response. Heather had considered Gus's only friend, his only companion in the world outside his family. Gus had never before asked to bring Angus to the house. Lester would have vetoed his request. But Lester was gone, they had lost him. The Cape was gone. Life had changed. Heather thought of their losses for ten seconds more and said, "Yes, of course."

She could only hope for the best. Was Lester looking down, shaking his head? Maybe, but he'd left her in charge, and she had to make the decisions now. Should she have instructed Gus to tell Angus to show up sober? What would Gert think? Clifford never said much about Angus, did he have a grudge against him too? She wasn't certain. And Marg, what would her reaction be? She suspected Gert would twist in her chair until she tied herself in knots, but that was Gert. However, Heather considered she had made the right decision, for Gus, for Angus, and for her.

The morning of the party, Heather made Gus have a bath and put on clean clothes as she decorated the table with paper horns and streamers around the room. She had to pick up the lobster in the morning. The party would start at two.

Gert and Clifford arrived first, Gert with presents and dessert. Marg had made squares, although Heather had a birthday cake already. They would have a lot to eat. Her parents and Marg left Spensers Island at the same time, taking separate vehicles. Marg seldom rode with Cliff and Gert. There was no escape from her mother then, if for some reason she had to get away, which she often did. Both vehicles passed Angus walking towards Lester's house. It was misty, but the morning's rain had mostly wound down to dribbles. Neither vehicle stopped to offer Angus a drive. Of course, they never dreamed he shared their destination. They wouldn't have believed it. Everyone knew of the man. What they knew was his shoddy reputation as a lobster thief. That's why they burned his boat. Not that the old tub was much good, but he got around in it. No one could work the motor but Angus, and he used it to skip up and down the coast.

It was strange about blame, Angus thought, watching the vehicles go by. He was no angel, but he was blamed for everything that happened along this coast, things he had never done. Not once had he taken a lobster from somebody's pot. He had taken his own, illegal fishing, yes, he was guilty. But the fact was, fishermen didn't like to see him out in the bay. Suspicious, they were, and they watched him like a hawk. That's why night on the water had been best for Angus. He liked to cut his motor if conditions were right and just listen to the sounds of the bay. The hum and squeal and haunting far-off cries. He would fish for flounder then, using shiny reflectors near his triple hooks to attract the fish.

Then he didn't have a boat anymore.

He made a meagre living. He could house paint but seldom got a job. So he lived rough, but still knew enough to bring a present for his buddy.

Gert and Cliff were already presenting their gifts to Gus. A hoodie with the words *Nova Scotia Strong* on the front. Heather had given him a new electric razor. Erik bought a new pair of work boots for Gus to wear to work in the new garden centre someday. Marg's gift was a new green sweater with gray trim.

Heather opened wine and it suddenly struck her. What should she offer Angus, should he actually show up? Angus was surely an alcoholic, and offering him wine might not be a good idea.

"Gussie, you'll look after Angus when he comes, okay?"

Twenty minutes later there was a soft knock at the door. Gus let Angus into the living room, taking the gift offered him in a brown paper bag. A new hatchet with a case for the belt.

"I knew you needed one," Angus said quietly. He and Gus sat in the corner by the small table where the birthday presents were spread out. Marg was talking to Heather in the kitchen and didn't see Angus when he arrived. Gert did, but thankfully didn't seem to recognize him. Her eyes only grew wide with surprise when Cliff said, "Hallo, Angus," giving Angus a friendly nod, passing him the peanuts.

Angus sat with Gus while he looked at his presents and they talked quietly to each other about trout fishing in winter. Heather served the wine, giving Gus and Angus Pepsi with ice.

Angus was far from complaining about anything. He was in a home with a family and had been invited to dinner. It didn't get any better.

Heather had sat the table for six and Gert stood over her watching.

"Six? There's five of us, why six place settings? Or is he"—she gave a slight flick of her head to indicate the corner where Angus was sitting—"staying for dinner too?"

"Yes," Heather said, "he's a friend of Gus's."

"You invited him?" Gert replied frostily. "Really, Heather, what were you thinking?"

Heather didn't feel she had to defend her decision to invite the outcast. She gave Gert a direct look and drew her into the kitchen, where she whispered, "It's Gus's birthday, he asked, and I said yes."

"But why?"

"Because Gus needs friends too."

"I see," Gert said. "So he's eating with us too?"

"Yes, of course he is."

"Most people wouldn't let the man in their house," Gert replied.

"I'm not most people," Heather answered.

Gert gave her a rueful look at said nothing more. Gert could see Heather had become somewhat more assertive lately, just like Marg, turning towards thirty and getting bossy. Gert drew in a deep breath. *These women*, she thought. *Why can't they be normal?*

There was no more said as they sat down at the table, with Angus the most nervous of the bunch. He was trying to watch how the others ate their salad and lobster. Did it matter what utensils he used? He usually tore a cooked lobster apart with his hands. He was relieved to see the others did the same. He simply wanted not to make any mistakes. He only hoped to be included, to fit into this family setting and not be noticed making some mistake in etiquette. But that Angus was there at all, seated at the family table, that was Heather's doing. He would not forget her kindness. It took all his courage just to come up to her, because he knew nothing of proper manners and less of saying thank you. But Angus wanted to make a good impression.

The meal went smoothly, and Cliff spoke a few words to Angus, passing him the butter or salad. Everyone said the lobster was delicious. Heather's cake, chocolate with boiled frosting, was Gus's favourite. They were now clearing the tables, Marg had out her fiddle, Gus had the spoons, and after a few tunes, including "Ned Landry's Happy Feet," one of Cliff's favourites, they had dessert of Cumberland County blueberries, ice cream, and birthday cake, the first Heather had made in years.

Heather was happy to see Marg also speaking to Angus. It was a decent thing to do, and Angus lit up when talking to her. Just a few kind words can make a difference.

Finally, the party was breaking up and Marg and her parents were heading home. At least Angus hadn't been totally ignored.

When they were out the door, Angus, with all the fortitude he could muster, came to Heather in the kitchen. He had not ventured, she noticed, out of the living room, even to use the washroom. Now he stood before her at the kitchen sink.

"I don't get invited out much," he stammered. They were standing face to face; he was an inch shorter than Heather, slightly looking up to her. She had never been close to him before. It was impossible to tell his age. His ruddy complexion showed the years of drink and abuse. There were fine lines running around under his eyes and deeper furrows making paths through his forehead. There wasn't an ounce of fat on the man. His skin was pulled tightly over his cheekbones. The frail face of a hungry man.

"I just want you to know how much I liked it. Being invited and seeing Gus's birthday presents and the good meal. Thank you very much."

Before Heather could respond, he was gone like a shot. She heard him say goodnight to Gus and the front door opened and then softly closed. *Wait*, she thought, *How will he get home? Angus lives in a cabin by Apple River Bay, that's more than fifteen kilometres away and it's already dark.* Heather ran out and called to him.

"Angus, how will you get home?"

"Walking," he replied.

"I'll drive you," she responded.

Gus was already asleep on the sofa with his birthday presents around him. She would scoot him to bed later.

She drove Angus down the dark road from Advocate Harbour to Apple River as the rain began. They drove mostly in silence, but the quiet was becoming uncomfortable, and Heather wanted to draw him out, to see if he was as smart as Gus said.

Then suddenly, Angus began talking. "Why do you think Lester never liked me? He liked almost everyone and everyone liked him. He caught me on the water once back in his fishing days and thought I was stealing his lobster, but I wasn't."

She hadn't expected such a declaration, hasn't expected to hear anything about Lester or his dislikes and likes. "Lester was a most forgiving man," Heather replied. "If he had got to know you some, he would have probably thought differently about you."

"I always respected him," Angus then surprisingly declared. They slowed, as there was some animal on the road up ahead. A fox, Angus said, given the way it scurried off into the bush. The rain suddenly came down hard, and for another ten minutes they didn't say a word.

"He was a good father, wasn't he?" Angus continued.

Heather was again startled. *What a strange question*, she thought. "Yes, he was a good father, but how did you know?"

"I watched him some with you guys at the Bar, and Gus told me. Lester looked after Gus really well, just like I do."

"I am glad to hear that. Gus takes things seriously even when they're not meant to be. I hope you're always kind to him."

"He's the only friend I've got, why would I ever mistreat him."

"I would like to consider myself your friend," she said, without exactly knowing why. Angus only looked at her, but there was something in his eyes, she thought. If there were words to say, he didn't have them.

She dropped him off at Apple River Bay and watched him make his way into the woods. When he got to the edge of the trees, he turned and waved goodnight to her. Heather then watched him disappear but didn't see him wipe tears from his eyes.

Driving back to Advocate Harbour, a feeling came over Heather, the same sensation she experienced immediately after her adventure on the water. A tingling sensation that told her she had done something good. Something worthwhile.

Chapter 18

Welcome News

Erik did everything he said he would. As the winter months passed, he stayed in Lester's bedroom. He and Heather got to know each other in the coastal manner, walking the beaches and along the Acadian dikes, searching for a piece of land for his small garden centre. He was staying and she was in love with him and the happiest she had ever felt. Surprisingly they found what they were looking for, right on route 209, just coming into Advocate Harbour. Erik said the location was perfect. You couldn't miss it, and there was room to expand.

Heather wondered if there was demand for a garden centre there, enough to justify the investment. But Erik said the investment was mostly hard work, and that he didn't plan to sell only locally, but supply other places. He hadn't wasted his time in Halifax or Saint John, he wasn't just sightseeing. He was also working, making contacts, meeting suppliers. He went to every plant nursery he could find and introduced himself anyplace that looked like it would sell blooming plants.

He realized he needed business cards but there was no business yet. All they had was a flat, open field, enthusiasm, the ability for hard work, and enough for two small greenhouses, one of which Erik would build himself with Gus's help.

Heather would work with him too. She marvelled at times how much she loved him. It was such a transition from how she felt about men a year ago. How it all happened so quickly. There was immense comfort in having Erik close.

On a sunny Sunday morning in April, Heather heard a knock on her door. There was Marg, whom she hadn't seen since Christmas. Marg had a wry smile on her face, quite unlike her usual expression. And she was waving a white envelope in her hand as she came inside.

"Surprise," she said. "Weren't expecting me, were you?"

"I didn't know you were even home."

"Well, I'm not, really. I arrived last night and I'm leaving now. Things became pretty uncomfortable in Spensers Island after I gave my parents this." Heather opened the envelope as they sat at the kitchen table.

Then Heather knew. Marg was going all the way. It was a wedding invitation. Margaret Jean Gilbert was to marry Gloria Dawn MacPhee in a civil ceremony in Halifax on June 19.

"Marg, you're really doing this?"

"I'm going all out to live my own life, no more beating around the bush, no more indecision. A full, lifelong commitment. So please be happy for me. And Heather, I wanted to ask you a favour." Marg paused, took a deep breath, and said, "Would you stand with me?"

"Of course I will. Oh Marg, are you certain about all this?"

"Heather, Mom is in a snit. I don't want my mother standing next to me at my wedding with a sour look on her face. Dad is uncomfortable, I know. Besides, I owe you. I haven't always been the best to you. But I am happy now. I'm not in a funk anymore. Please come and stand by your friend, who is a cur sometimes and isn't always so friendly."

Heather walked around the table and embraced Marg. "I'm so happy for you, Marg. If you've found happiness, good for you. It can be an elusive thing. But Marg, we've both finally found it."

She didn't tell Marg of her own plans, that she and Erik would be married in the autumn. That could wait. This was Marg's day and there would be no one spoiling it. She had saved Erik and she was keeping him.

"I wish you and Gloria all the happiness in the world. It's a strange thing about happiness, how it arrives, sometimes like a soft wind and at times like a hurricane. Something I thought I'd never experience, to have a man in my life. Now I'm overflowing, and why not? I'm in love and, I finally got my discharge papers from the military. They have given me a voluntary release, there is nothing negative in it, so that's a mighty relief."

Her release had arrived two days ago. Erik was standing behind her with his hands on her shoulders as Heather opened the papers with shaky hands. When she read the words *voluntary release,* she turned and pressed herself against him in a triumphant embrace. Aside from Erik, Marg was the first to know that Heather's long wait was over. She wanted to keep the happy relief bottled up inside for a while. It was personal; she just wanted to hold on to it.

They sat for a few moments and Marg turned serious. "I hate to ask you this, it's only you I can ask. If you can, please convince my parents to come to the wedding. Mum said she wouldn't, but Dad will, even if she doesn't." A rather rueful smile came to Marg's lips. "Knowing Gert, she's too nosey not to attend. But she's in her aggravation mode right now, so I can't talk to her."

"I'll do my best with Gert," Heather replied.

Chapter 19

New Beginnings

Marg and Gloria tied the knot at Gloria's beautifully decorated home in Halifax. Even Gert was impressed with the interior of the house and much relieved when she learned her daughter and partner planned to adopt children.

"There will be grandchildren after all," Gert said to Heather during the small reception. *Maybe grandnieces and nephews too*, Heather thought. She and Erik had plans too, but they were withholding their plans because this was Marg's big day, and maybe Marg had never had enough of the limelight, and Heather had had too much.

Heather was incredibly happy. She and Erik agreed to a quiet ceremony in the little church in Advocate Harbour. Gus would stand with the bride; Erik had bought him a spiffy new blue serge suit. Erik's mother and uncle were coming from Norway. But it was Advocate, after all, and although they had planned a quiet wedding, word got around. Heather suspected Gert had talked, even probably called the newspapers. She could hear Gert telling reporters, "Yes it's true, the hero of the Cobequid coast is marrying the man she had saved. Great story, eh?"

They were all over the news, a week before the wedding. All over again, and the media showed up in droves. There were three television cameras with lights, their cables sprawling across the churchyard. Radio reporters and newspapers too. Heather had been told more than once that in a changing and difficult world, people needed happy stories more than ever, and here was a good one.

The newlyweds avoided more publicity by honeymooning in Norway. Erik wanted to show her his country of birth. She loved Norway and loved her guide and husband.

*

It was the winter storm of 2021, called the second White Juan, that took out the float house. The shingles blew off one by one, resembling wounded birds flapping into the whiteness of the blizzard. The rest of the structure was pushed into Apple River Bay, which was so gorged at the time, so high on frothy seawater, it was up to the shanty's door. The float house was carried around the finger into the wider Chignecto Bay and down the coast into waters unknown. As if one could not live without the other, the exceptionally high spring tides took out the dance floor too, as if its job was done here. The children had grown up and gone, and it was no longer needed. Unlike the shanty, which went quickly, the old dance the floor bobbed around for days, one corner sticking out of the water, revealed as a half-hidden invitation to haul it ashore, where there were children. But no one did. Finally, as if tired of waiting, the floor floated down the coast.

Lester and the family had had fun with it, Gert said, a free summer cottage for many years. They all agreed it was the best of times with those cookouts and dances on that old floor.

There would be another float house on the Bar, Erik promised Heather. Cliff said he was ready to assist, but then smirked. "I have another job to do first."

Heather noticed Erik was smiling too but trying to hide it. "What are you two up to?" she asked but got no reasonable reply.

It was a whirlwind summer for Heather and Erik with marriage and travel and settling into their new lives and a new business. Erik was building one greenhouse himself. He had borrowed money from the bank for the larger one. September arrived before they knew it. A few weeks later back in her teaching job, Heather was buoyant driving home. A particular happiness reserved for the young in love.

Arriving home, she saw Cliff's truck in her driveway and Cliff, in his carpenter's apron, had started construction on some sort of building.

"It's Lester's surprise for you," Cliff announced. "It was all Lester's idea. I suppose anything to keep you here. He would do anything for you and Gus."

They had planned where to put it, just on the other side of the driveway. What could be more convenient? Lester had cooked this up and paid for it, Cliff said, a combined art studio and gallery. Heather would have a place to display and sell her paintings. Cliff had studied what was needed for the windows in such a facility. Heather smiled to herself when he said the lighting was very important; reflection and such. They had given this project a fair amount of thought and consideration in the last months of Lester's life. Heather wasn't certain she was given the entire truth about payment, but Cliff looked hurt when questioned about it.

"Would I lie to you?" he said, as he often said with one of his tall stories. She stood back and visualized the finished product, just as the newest member of her family drove into the yard. Erik had gone for nails and screws. Heather was suddenly flooded with emotion.

This is my family, she thought, *and a damn good one at that.*

*

On a warm December day, a week after her birthday and two years after she had rescued a man from death, almost three years since she had left the army, Heather walked up to the store in the village. It was there she passed the newspaper stand. The headline stopped her in her tracks.

Armed Forces to end its jurisdiction over sexual crimes, but change won't happen "overnight": Anand

Dec 13, 2022

Defence Minister Anita Anand says she has directed the Canadian Armed Forces to end its jurisdiction over the response to sexual offences. (Canadian Press, 2022)

Heather picked up the paper. Her hands trembled slightly as a long line of memories swept through her in quick succession. She still had tremors sometimes, and bad dreams too, but far less since she had found romantic love, the goodness of life and the healing by the big waters of the Fundy coast. She picked up the newspaper. *Maybe, just maybe, it won't happen to others*, she thought.

Maybe it will never happen to anyone again.

She stood in that store and wondered if she was truly one of the last to be so affected by her own army. *Maybe*, she thought.

Maybe.

Acknowledgements

A note of thanks to the people who assisted with this story. Dr. David Howe of Parrsboro who made a significant contribution with his medical knowledge. Karine McGregor has been my first proofreader through my books since *Diligent River Daughter*. And of course, my publisher Vanda Jackson of Purple Porcupine Publishing. Also, my support at home by my wife Helen. Thank you all.

Bruce Graham

Works Cited

Newspaper headline on page 168: Canadian Press, December 13, 2022. Video, "Newsroom Ready: Armed Forces to end its jurisdiction over sexual crimes, but change won't happen 'overnight': Anand." Unique identifier CP165515868. Accessed October 7, 2024 https://www.cpimages.com/archive/Newsroom-Ready--Armed-Forces-to-end-its-jurisdiction-over-sexual-crimes--but-change-won-t-happen--overnight---Anand-2RLQZBRY0HPRN.html

About the Author

Bruce Graham has always been drawn to the rugged beauty of Nova Scotia's coastline—especially the Minas Basin and the Minas Channel of the Bay of Fundy. As a child, he spent endless hours exploring the shore. "I loved writing this book," Graham says. "Maybe because the coast is part of me. It certainly shaped my early life."

An accomplished writer, Graham has authored a dozen books, with three adapted for the stage. His storytelling is backed by an award-winning career in broadcasting. A graduate with honors from the Radio and Television Arts program at Cambridge School in Boston, he has earned three prestigious awards: a Lifetime Achievement Award from the Canadian Radio & Television News Directors Association, the Ohio State University Award for journalistic excellence, and an Atlantic Journalism Award for his widely respected nightly television commentary, *The Final Word.*